MOUSE MISSION

ALSO BY PRUDENCE BREITROSE

Mousenet

Mousemobile

MOUSE MISSION

by prudence breitrose

illustrated by stephanie yue

Disney • HYPERION

LOS ANGELES   NEW YORK

Printed in the United States of America
First Edition, October 2015
1 3 5 7 9 10 8 6 4 2
FAC-020093-15196
Reinforced binding

Library of Congress Cataloging-in-Publication Data
Breitrose, Prudence E.
Mouse mission / by Prudence Breitrose ; illustrated by Stephanie Yue.—First edition.
pages cm
Sequel to: Mousemobile.
Summary: "When a timber company threatens to cut down the rain forest on the
island of Marisco, Megan's mom leads the effort to save it, with the help of the Mouse
Nation. The mission takes the family (and mice) to England, where the trail leads
to a duke's palace full of dangerous humans—and helpful British mice"—Provided by
publisher.
ISBN 978-1-4847-1117-0
[1. Rain forests—Fiction. 2. Conservation of natural resources—Fiction.
3. Kidnapping—Fiction. 4. Mice—Fiction.] I. Yue, Stephanie, illustrator. II. Title.
PZ7.B84895Ml 2015
[Fic]—dc23   2014039009

Visit www.DisneyBooks.com

SUSTAINABLE FORESTRY INITIATIVE   Certified Sourcing
www.sfiprogram.org
SFI-00993

THIS LABEL APPLIES TO TEXT STOCK

For Henry

chapter one

S he could have been any sixth grader in Cleveland pedaling home from school, except for the mouse holding tight to a red braid that stuck out below her helmet.

And except for the fact that her lips were moving, though there was no sign of a phone.

"Suppose I don't want to do it?" she was saying.

"C'mon," said the mouse. "You have to. You're the most famous human in the world. Or has that fact slipped your mind?"

"Maybe I don't want to be famous," she said.

"It's a bit late for that, isn't it?" he said crisply. "Maybe you should have thought of it just a *leeetle* bit sooner."

"Grrr," she growled. Yes, Trey was her best friend—of any species—but he really knew how to push her buttons, in this case by sounding just like her mom. Megan decided to annoy him back by taking him literally.

"So when you talked to me in the night last year, I shouldn't have made friends with you. I shouldn't have gone to Headquarters to sign that Treaty Between the Species. I shouldn't have helped the Mouse Nation get computers. Because I should have known where it would all lead—that I'd have to go on a dumb television show so millions of mice . . ."

"Go on," he said.

"*Billions* of mice . . ."

"Go *on*," he said again.

"Can gawk at me . . ."

"And, and, and?" he prompted.

"And I'll go red," she said.

"Yesssss!" said Trey. She could feel a tug on her braid, as if someone was shifting his grip so he could rub his paws together in glee.

It was such a big deal, for mice, when her face turned red. They were overawed by the sight of a mammal—a real mammal, not just some reptile—changing color. In their amazement, mice completely forgot their manners and gawked, and pointed, and made the sign for "Laughing out loud." Now the leader of the Mouse Nation, known behind his back as the Big Cheese, wanted her to give a speech on Megan Day to every mouse in the world, all of them gawking and pointing and laughing because of course she'd blush.

Yes, it made sense for the Big Cheese to celebrate Megan Day, the anniversary of her visit to the Headquarters of the Mouse Nation in Silicon Valley. It made sense to celebrate the signing of that famous Treaty Between the Species, which promised she'd help mice get tiny Thumbtop computers in exchange for their help on climate change. It made sense to celebrate the way mice had carried out that promise in Operation Cool It, secretly encouraging politicians and opinion makers and captains of industry and just plain folks to use less energy.

But did the Big Cheese's gala show to celebrate the treaty have to include a live speech from his favorite human?

"Maybe the show won't happen," she said. "Maybe something more important will come along and they'll drop it. Some crisis."

"Hey, careful what you wish for," said her braid. "Don't you think we've all had enough excitement for one year?"

And yes, looking back on last summer, when the entire Headquarters of the Mouse Nation had to escape from California in the Mousemobile, Trey was right. That was quite enough excitement for one year.

Megan was not the only mammal to have doubts about the Megan Day show that afternoon. The Big Cheese had doubts too.

When he had first decided to organize a celebration, he'd imagined something quiet and dignified, because, as he often said, the fact that mice were so small made it especially important for them to act with dignity.

There'd be an ode to Miss Megan written by Talking Mouse Five—Sir Quentin—who'd recently been appointed Mouse Laureate. A speech from the Big Cheese. Maybe a short video about mouse success around the world, like the good work of Swedish mice in reducing that country's demand for electricity. Maybe a short documentary on the hundreds of mice who had volunteered to toil in the factory at Planet Mouse, assembling Thumbtops. Maybe a segment on the solar blobs that mice fashioned into jewelry, making enough money to cover everyone's expenses. And of course the climax: a live speech from Miss Megan, the most famous human in the world.

That was before Talking Mouse Seven got involved. Savannah.

She hadn't been the Big Cheese's first choice as host for the show. He'd really wanted Trey—a competent talking mouse who would never embarrass his species. But Trey had totally flunked his screen test. He'd looked at the wrong camera. He'd mumbled his lines. He'd stared down at his paws. He'd been, in short, terrible.

The Big Cheese suspected that Trey had failed the test on purpose because of the strong bond that exists among talking mice, the handful who'd been born with the sort of mouth that can be trained to make human sounds. And he suspected (rightly, as it happened) that Trey wanted Savannah to have the job, because if ever there was a mouse made for showbiz . . .

But recently the Big Cheese had heard disturbing rumors about the show, and this afternoon he'd asked to watch a rehearsal.

His heart sank as Savannah sashayed onto the set on her hind feet, swiveling her hips to make her tail swoosh from side to side. Tweaking the brim of a purple hat. Sweeping off her sunglasses as she sat on a doll-size couch, her tail draped over its arm.

"Mouselings!" she breathed, in a voice straight from Hollywood. "Mouselings of the world! Welcome to our gala celebration. Welcome to Megan Day!"

Then Savannah leapt up from the couch to do a pirouette, her long necklace flying wide.

"Put your paws together," she breathed, "for your very own Mousettes!"

A row of young mice appeared, girl mice with little pink frills around their waists like human skirts. They waved pompoms in unison while Savannah trilled, "Come on, girls! Give me an M! Give me an O! Give me a U!"

The Big Cheese could hardly bear to watch.

It was partly his fault, he thought, for letting Savannah

violate one of his strictest rules—the one stating that no mouse should adopt human clothes and customs like the mice in so many children's books.

But it was Savannah's fault too, wasn't it? For being such a hero last summer? Risking death by hawk as she saved his entire Headquarters staff from certain destruction? After that, it was hard to insist that she act like a mouse, and look like a mouse, particularly when some of the five Humans Who Knew encouraged her, buying her new doll hats and necklaces and handbags, because she made them laugh.

The Mousettes had formed a wobbly pyramid, but apparently they'd stacked up one layer too many, because the whole thing collapsed, causing young mice to cascade all over the floor. Savannah froze as the Big Cheese made the sign for "Aaargh" in the silent language most mice use. (For "Aaargh," you bow your head and press the backs of your front paws to your forehead.)

Then he turned to the Director of Media, sitting beside him, and said, "We have to talk."

He led the director out of the studio and into one of the hundreds of cubicles that made up the Cleveland Headquarters of the Mouse Nation.

"The treaty we signed last year, on that first Megan Day," he said. "Did it say anything about mouse pyramids?"

"No, it didn't, actually," said the director, who like most mice had a very literal mind. "But it didn't say mice *couldn't* make pyramids."

His boss was speechless. Could it really be happening? That Savannah's way of thinking had spread to his *directors*? To members of his Mouse Council?

Savannah had followed them into the tiny cubicle, filling it to the bursting point with her big-brimmed hat.

"Is there a problem, sir?" she asked. "Because you've hardly seen anything yet. Like the Youth Chorus? And our groovy sports report with Larry? You remember him, my friend Cleveland Mouse 42? Then we have a stand-up comedy mouse and an animal impersonator and—"

"How many times have you heard me say that as a small species, we need dignity? Gravitas?" the Big Cheese interrupted, feeling at a disadvantage because Savannah was so close that it was hard for him to express himself properly in Mouse Sign Language, or MSL for short. "We must above all maintain our mouseness. Not slavishly imitate the larger species."

"Oh please, please, pretty please?" begged Savannah. She tried to go down on one knee, which mice can't do, not having the right sort of knees, so she crouched, with her hat taking up even more room.

The Big Cheese tried to glare at her, but there was something about Savannah, especially when she fluttered her eyelashes. Something that made it hard to hurt her feelings. And he sort of caved.

"I will consider the future of this extravaganza," he said, "after I watch the rest of it."

They went back to their places in the studio, where the Youth Chorus was ready to lurch into song in Mouse Sign Language, their tails and ears and paws swaying and bobbing in unison. They got through the first part:

Hail our Nation, doubly hail.
Mice now rule, from tip to tail.
We are billions, we are smart,
We no longer are apart.
As each mouse son and each mouse daughter
Keeps the world from growing hotter . . .

But then one by one the young mice stopped their signs and stared at the mouse who had rushed into the studio with a message for the Big Cheese.

"Danger," he said in MSL. "Your humans. They're out of control."

chapter two

Megan had just passed Uncle Fred's house, marked with a plaque that read BIRTHPLACE OF THE THUMBTOP, when she got the first sign of trouble. Trey's sharp ears had picked up a beep from the tiny computer in a pocket of Megan's backpack. He scuttled down to read an e-mail that had just come in from Julia—one of the mice who had been with Megan ever since she learned about the Mouse Nation.

"Uh-oh," he said, as he came back up to Megan's shoulder. "Mom alert."

"She's *home*?" said Megan. She braked and stopped with one foot on the edge of the sidewalk. "So early? Just so she can keep bugging me?"

"She wasn't exactly *bugging* you was she, last night?" asked Trey. "More like hinting?"

"Well maybe, but with hints like that . . ."

The hinting/bugging had gotten worse since her mom had married Jake, and his son, Joey—Megan's step-cousin—was promoted to stepbrother. Not that there was anything wrong with Joey. Megan liked him a lot, most of the time. It was the comparison problem. Her mom would never actually come out and say, "Why can't you be more like Joey?" But you could tell that's what she was thinking sometimes, especially on the matter of making human friends. Joey's life was rich in teams and clubs and people to hang out with, while Megan's life was mostly rich in mice.

The topic of Getting Involved and Making Friends had come up again last night, when Savannah had been telling the humans about the Megan Day show in general, and the Mousettes in particular. She loved, loved, loved those Mousettes. Megan's mom hadn't actually said anything about Mousettes, or about cheerleaders, because she didn't need to. She just gave Megan a look, and smiled, and raised one eyebrow, but her meaning was obvious enough to make Joey and his dad laugh.

"Mom, there is no *way* I could ever make cheerleader," Megan had said. And the "Why can't you have a normal social life like Joey" conversation had ended there, in laughter. But not forever. When Megan was on her way to bed, Susie Fisher made a point of saying, "Okay, kiddo, so you don't want to be a cheerleader, but you know what? It's really not healthy to go through life without human friends. Let's have a nice long talk tomorrow afternoon, as soon as I get home."

But did it have to be right now? Megan would much rather follow her usual afternoon routine, starting with her daily lesson in MSL from Julia, who was her second best friend among mice. Then Trey would help her with her math, because he was much better at it than she was. But instead she'd have to spend an hour or so trying to keep her mom from pushing her into a computer club or the Girl Scouts or a soccer team or something.

"Maybe we should go to the library and do my homework there," she suggested, slowing up. "We'll find a corner where no one can see you helping me."

But it was one of those times when Trey (who was after all full grown) talked to her like an adult.

"You'd only postpone the discussion," he said. "Best to get it over, so . . . wait."

He must have heard another beep, because he climbed down to read the new message on the Thumbtop's tiny screen.

"What's up now?" Megan asked when he came back.

"Not good," he said. "It's from Julia again and she's frantic. Your mom's freaking out. Big problem with the poem."

"The *poem*?"

"Sir Quentin's poem. His ode for Megan Day. Better get home fast, because Julia says your mom . . ."

"Something to do with *Sir Quentin*?"

Sir Quentin had come by their house yesterday to recite his ode.

"It would be a privilege," he had said, "if Miss Susie could hear my poor verse and perchance provide guidance on any couplets that stray from my desired meter of iambic pentameters."

"Iambic pedometers?" Joey had interrupted, with a grin. Like Megan, he sometimes found Sir Quentin a pain because this was a Talking Mouse who had learned to speak with the help of historical dramas from British television and never used a short word when a long one would do.

"Pent*ameters*," Sir Quentin corrected him. "The meter beloved by the Bard. By which I mean of course Shakespeare."

"How long is it?" Susie had asked.

"A true epic may require many hours to read," Sir Quentin had said. "However, at the request of my leader I have limited myself to verses that will take no more than eight minutes to deliver."

He'd begun to recite them last night, standing up on his hind legs, his iambic pentameters marching relentlessly out:

All hail that glorious and important day
When mice and humans jointly found a way
To heal the ills of our poor planet Earth
With brains and brawn and yes, a little mirth
When fair Miss Megan to Headquarters came
To there ensure we'd never be the same . . .

It was at that point that Susie jumped in to say it sounded wonderful but if it was really eight minutes long maybe he could e-mail it to her and she'd go through it when she had the time.

And now—well, now what?

"D'you think she hated that poem but she doesn't dare tell Sir Quentin?" Megan suggested now.

"Julia didn't say, but it sounds worse than that," Trey said. "Much worse. Please! Just pedal!"

He held on tight while Megan cranked up her speed and raced the next couple of blocks, past the big house with a sign reading:

PLANET MOUSE
Home of the Thumbtop,
made in Cleveland by mice

After that, there were only two more corners to navigate to her own house, which Uncle Fred had named "The Fishery" because everyone in it except Megan was now a Fisher. It had been a great find, with its perfect location right behind Planet Mouse and connected with its yard by a gate in the back fence.

Susie Fisher's car was in the driveway, its door hanging open. Not a good sign. Megan closed the car door as she passed, dumped her bike on its side, and ran to the front door, which opened from the inside just as she reached it.

A look at her mom's face told Megan that this was going to be bad. Yes, she'd seen her mom angry before, but seldom like this.

There was a skittering of feet on the kitchen floor, then Julia ran up to Megan's shoulder. And Julia was trembling, as mice sometimes do when human emotions are running high.

After a quick nuzzle against Megan's neck, Julia jumped onto the kitchen table, where she made some urgent-looking gestures in MSL, including a couple Megan had just learned. "Danger." "Stop her."

"What happened?" asked Megan.

"Look!" said her mom, pointing at her laptop. "Just look! I'm going to kill them."

"Who?" asked Megan.

"The Big Cheese," said her mom, running a hand through her springy fair hair. "And Sir Quentin. Because if this is what we get for trusting another species . . . The Big Cheese knows how important it is. But do you know what they've done, your precious mice? They've leaked some very secret information. Now the whole project is in danger!"

"What, the rain forest thing?" asked Megan.

"Yes. That one chance we had to save it." Her mom was almost crying, and Megan ran to give her a hug.

This was one of the weirdest environmental campaigns Susie Fisher had ever been involved with. It was a huge deal, involving a stretch of rain forest on Marisco, an island in the Indian Ocean. This was one of the last forests on that part of the planet that was still completely wild, and it had been kept that way by the government of Marisco until recently, when a group of generals seized power. A month ago, mice had found a document on the generals' computers—a document that revealed their plan to sell the rights to the forest to Loggocorp, a huge international timber company.

"Maybe they won't cut it all down," Megan had said when her mom first got the news. "Maybe they'll just take out a tree here and there."

"What, log selectively?" said her mom. "Sustainably?

Loggocorp doesn't know what those words mean! They're the worst. They clear-cut, every time."

She had sent the news about the generals' plans to a rain forest expert named Sir Brian Mason, a professor at London University. Sir Brian, in turn, got in touch with the ex-president of Marisco, the man the generals had kicked out—and the ex-president gave him a message of hope. According to a local legend that had passed down through many generations, a Mariscan ruler long ago gave the rights to the Western Forest to a mysterious Englishman, known only as Coconut Man.

"All we have to do is find who Coconut Man was," said Susie one night at dinner. "And locate some of his descendants. Then those guys can claim the forest. Keep it away from Loggocorp. Keep it wild."

Her husband, Jake, had hooted with laughter.

"Coconut Man!" he said. "Really? Hey, why don't I save you some time and say he was one of *my* ancestors? So I can claim the forest."

"Well, obviously his descendants will need proof!" said Susie. "Some sort of deed to show they own the rights."

"And Sir Brian will find that proof, right?" said Jake. "Written on a leaf? Or carved on a coconut?"

"It could happen!" said Susie. "We have mice on our side, remember?"

Indeed, when there are billions of mice throughout the world who can overhear any human conversation, and search through any stack of papers, and read the documents on any computer, it is good to have them on your side.

The Big Cheese reported on the search for Coconut Man at one of the regular meetings that he held with his humans every Tuesday. It was great news. Hunting through the old palace archives, mice in Marisco had indeed found the identity of Coconut Man. Mice in England had dug up the name of at least one of his descendants—someone who could speak for the whole family.

"Does that guy have a name?" Jake had asked. "That descendant?"

Yes, but not one that the Big Cheese was ready to reveal.

"I am sure you will understand," he said, "that the name of the family must be kept secret from Loggocorp at all costs. In my experience it's easiest for humans to keep secrets if they don't know them in the first place."

And that was all they could get.

Susie told Sir Brian as much as she could. That he should summon a group of experts—and the ex-president of Marisco—to a meeting place near London. From there—thanks to Susie's mysterious contacts—they'd be taken to meet Coconut Man's descendant, so they could persuade him to claim the forest, and keep it wild.

"But now look!" said Susie. "It's a disaster!"

Megan peered at her mom's laptop, covered in iambic pentameters:

> *Miss Susie, too—and can we ask for more?*
> *Is working to protect Marisco's shore,*
> *An island where—oh, spare the woodsman's ax!*
> *To save the forest we must not be lax.*
> *Let loggers now not trash Marisco's lands*
> *Where many rare lemurs do roam in bands!*
> *Are coconuts important in this plot?*
> *Dread Loggocorp must hope that they are not!*
> *Sir Brian's meeting soon, is our belief,*
> *In secret will to forests bring relief.*

"Now Sir Quentin's told the whole world about that meeting," said Susie, her voice shaking. "Loggocorp will be watching Sir

Brian all the time, hoping to find out who that guy is—Coconut Man's great-great-grandson or whatever. Then, who knows—they might offer his family millions of dollars to give up their claim to the forest before they even hear Sir Brian's proposal!"

Megan sighed with relief, because if it was only Sir Quentin, there was nothing scary there, surely. Nothing bad can happen if the only guys who learn your secrets are mice, because of that line in the treaty, the one that reads:

* Mice will never hurt humans.

There was no way mice would tell Loggocorp about secret plans to find Coconut Man's descendants, and their claim to the forest, because that would hurt the humans who were trying to save it. Not to mention the lemurs that lived there.

Megan couldn't blame her mom for being worried, of course. After all, it had been only a couple of months since she became the fifth Human Who Knew that mice had evolved. She was still learning to trust them.

"It's okay," she explained. "Sir Quentin can't tell any humans about your plans because . . ."

"Because of your precious treaty?" asked her mom. "So what do you make of *this!*"

She pulled her phone out of her bag, clicked on it, and held it out to Megan. Her hand was trembling a bit, which made it hard for Megan to read the text, so she took the phone out of her mom's hands to peer at the screen—and felt her own trust in mice take a hit.

The message was from someone called Doug. Her mom had mentioned him before—a biologist who worked for Loggocorp and hated what the company did to rain forests. Hated it so much that he'd started leaking information to Megan's mom. This time he had texted:

Bosses know about meeting in England.

"And you think they found out from Sir *Quentin?*" Megan asked.

"Well, how else? From that dreadful poem! Maybe he put it online for everyone to see. Made a mistake with the privacy settings."

"Mice don't make mistakes!" Megan wailed.

Her mom usually listened to her on the subject of mice, but not this time.

"Well, they just did. And I'm going up to Headquarters right now to ask your Big Cheese and Sir Quentin to explain themselves, and if they don't, then I will personally wring their necks."

"Mom, you can't! You can't just go up to Headquarters!"

Indeed, it had been one of the first rules the Big Cheese had set up when he moved his Headquarters to the second floor of Planet Mouse a couple of months ago. No humans should ever penetrate his space except for the regular visits of Mr. Joey and Miss Megan, who took turns going just as far as the upstairs bathroom to empty the poop-tray, top up the water in the drinking fountain that Uncle Fred had invented for the mice, and leave fresh bags of mouse food.

There was no way to explore beyond the bathroom, because a phalanx of muscle mice armed with toothpicks always blocked their path, keeping humans out of the bedrooms where two thousand mice worked on their Thumbtop computers. Besides, there'd be no room in those bedrooms for human feet. Using pieces of balsa wood that Uncle Fred had cut for them, the mice had absolutely covered the floor space with a complex labyrinth of tiny cubicles and offices.

"Wish you could see it," Trey had said one day. "It's amazing. Even we get lost up there."

And now, would Susie Fisher actually storm past the guards? Crunch those balsa wood offices underfoot? Stomp on mice as she rampaged through Headquarters, looking for Sir Quentin and the Big Cheese?

chapter three

There was only one person Megan could think of who might slow her mom down, might keep her from roaring up the stairs at Planet Mouse to Headquarters.

"Let's ask Jake—" she began, but got nowhere.

"Oh, you think that just because I'm married now I need a *man* to take over?" said her mom, heading out the back door. "I didn't exactly promise to obey him. Give me a break!"

She set off briskly down the path that led to the gate in the fence, and beyond it, Planet Mouse. The best Megan could do was to sprint ahead with Trey and Julia on her shoulders, reaching the other house just ahead of her mom so Trey could run up to Headquarters with his warning: Danger. Your humans are out of control.

Megan dashed into the office where Jake and Uncle Fred

supervised the production of Thumbtops and their distribution to mice all over the world.

"What the . . ." said Jake, seeing her face.

"It's Mom," said Megan. "Stop her, stop her, stop her!"

Megan was just in time. Jake was waiting as Susie came into Planet Mouse, the massive figure of Uncle Fred just behind him. And yes, Jake did convince Susie to at least flop on the couch in the big front office instead of running up the stairs.

It all poured out. Sir Quentin's poem. The leak about Sir Brian's meeting. The need to find out what role mice had played. The need for vengeance.

Jake was great at calming Susie down, far better than Uncle Fred, who was her younger brother so she never seemed to take him seriously, even though he was twice her size. Jake persuaded her to wait and at least give the Big Cheese twenty minutes to prepare his defense and explain what was going on.

Julia and Trey took that message upstairs to the Headquarters television studio, where the Big Cheese went into "deadly calm" mode—the total stillness that told his followers he was thinking at lightning speed.

"Come," was all he said in response to Julia's message. "Follow me."

The Big Cheese led Julia and Trey to the little office that

had been set up for Sir Quentin when he was appointed Mouse Laureate, its walls decorated with pictures of human poets. Beneath their gaze sat a mouse who looked as if the stuffing had been knocked out of him.

"I meant no harm!" he protested, when the Big Cheese demanded an explanation. "Oh sir, how could you suspect that with all the admiration I feel toward our human collaborators—with all the reverence I display—"

"I simply want to know," the Big Cheese interrupted, with slow, careful gestures, "whether a copy of your poem could have leaked into hostile hands."

"Leaked? Not by me," said Sir Quentin. "My electronic version was of course behind the firewall" (the security system that kept all but five humans away from the Nation's Web site). "If any lines perchance reached hostile eyes, it could have been only after Miss Susie received the e-mail to which the poem was attached. Is it not possible that she printed up my ode and proudly showed it to colleagues who appreciate a good iambic pentameter? And that one of them . . ."

"You *e-mailed* your poem to Miss Susie?" the Big Cheese interrupted.

"Indeed, at her request," said Sir Quentin. "I had hoped to entertain her with a full recitation yesterday, but she asked that I transmit my epic electronically in order that she might peruse it at her leisure and perhaps identify any quatrains that were less than felicitous."

There was silence—stillness—as Trey and Julia gazed at their leader, looking for warning signs. But the Big Cheese kept his icy calm.

"Send the Director of Security to my office," he ordered to a messenger mouse, then turned to Trey. "Go inform our humans that in eighteen minutes I will join them so that together we may lift the burden of suspicion from this mouse. And from us."

. . . .

It wasn't at all like the regular Tuesday meetings between the Big Cheese and the five Humans Who Knew.

For one thing, there were only four humans, because Joey was out doing whatever Joey did. And another thing: normally, the humans who lined up on the office couch were clean and pressed, because that's the way the leader of the mouse world liked it. Today there hadn't really been time for the clean-and-pressed bit, and as often happened in the afternoons, Uncle Fred's T-shirt showed traces of lunch.

It was Megan who went upstairs to fetch the little old bird-cage that had originally served as a fake prison for mice but had since become a ceremonial mouse-throne and transport device. Today the Big Cheese had asked one other mouse to climb in with him, a mouse with the red thread around his neck that marked him as a director, a member of the Mouse Council.

Usually Sir Quentin rode in the cage to act as interpreter, but the Big Cheese was afraid that the sight of him might enrage Miss Susie. So it was Trey who translated, as the humans watched the leader of the Mouse Nation for any hint of his mood. Was there a droop of the ears that could mean embarrassment, an acknowledgment that the Mouse Nation had goofed? Was there a twitch of the tail that could mean anger? No, the Big Cheese stood tall in his cage, looking at them with the confidence of a mouse in control.

"As you all know," he began, "this rain forest project is dear to the hearts of mice. We know the benefits of preserving the forest, on so many levels. It was an unfortunate coincidence that Talking Mouse Five referred to Sir Brian's meeting in his ode just as the timber company was hearing about it from human sources."

"Human sources?" said Susie sharply. "Not from Sir Brian's group, that's for sure! No way they would have told anybody!"

The Big Cheese bowed in her direction. "I agree that it was unlikely that they made such a disclosure voluntarily," he said. "I defer to my Director of Security for an explanation."

The director shuffled to the front of the cage.

"The generals in charge of Marisco routinely hack into the computer of ex-President Pindoran, whom they suspect of plotting to regain power. On one of those occasions they must have come across some correspondence with Sir Brian and the other experts with whom he has conferred. Their e-mail addresses were, we believe, passed to Loggocorp. Now their e-mail is probably being hacked. And their cell phones."

"Mine too?" squeaked Susie.

"Yours too," said the director.

Megan's mom was leaning forward, her face in her hands. Then she looked up, with a sad smile at the Big Cheese. "We can't win, can we?" she said.

"Of course you can win!" he said. "With mice on your side, how could you lose? We will put all our efforts into ensuring that from now on, plans for preservation of the forest can be carried out in secret."

"But they'll just keep hacking, won't they?" said Susie. "They'll find out even more about the meeting in London. They'll stalk Sir Brian's group."

"For which reason," said the Big Cheese, "you should take certain steps, now."

He spelled out what the humans should do. Get a message to the ex-president of Marisco and all the rain forest experts, right now. Tell them that until further notice there should be no more mention of the Western Forest of Marisco, nor of Coconut Man, nor of the meeting in England, on their phones or computers.

"How on earth can we send them that message," said Susie, "if they're already being hacked?"

"Fortunately, according to our informants," replied the Big Cheese, "the phones of your experts' spouses have not yet been tampered with. I suggest that you borrow Mr. Fred's phone to call them, perhaps starting with Sir Brian's wife, Lady Valerie."

Megan was glad to see the beginning of a smile on her mom's face.

"You know their wives, their partners?" Susie said. "I suppose you know their telephone numbers?"

The Big Cheese bowed slightly, as if accepting a compliment. He pointed to the Thumbtop that an IT mouse had been working on at the back of the cage, and Trey read the telephone numbers off its screen for Susie to call. One by one, Susie secretly left a message for each expert: Heinrich, the zoologist from Germany; Martin, the climatologist from Ghana; Pierre, the French botanist. And Laura, the lemur lady from Australia.

There could be no more communication about the rain forest until they all gathered at a hotel near the London airport. From there, the group would be taken to a secure location where they would work on their proposal. When the guy from Coconut Man's family showed up, they'd be ready to make the presentation that could save the forest.

After Susie had made the last call, she sank back into the cushions of the couch, her eyes closed.

"Do you know which humans are doing the actual hacking?" Uncle Fred asked the Director of Security.

"For legal reasons, it's unlikely to be Loggocorp employees," said the director. "They probably prefer to keep their hands clean, as it were. We think that they are using independent hackers—hackers for hire. I've queried the mice whose job it is to keep track of the most prominent networks of hackers— people who might provide such a service."

"Like Faceless?" asked Uncle Fred, his beard dropping south.

Megan remembered seeing something on television about Faceless and the thousands of hackers who went under that name, including some who had found their way into the most secure government computers.

"Indeed," said the director. "Faceless has recently made a change in its goals, its stated aims. Until now they hacked for their own entertainment, to demonstrate their power. But now I am informed that they do it for money."

"Hacking for hire," said Susie in a small voice. "For Loggocorp."

"Have no fear," said the Big Cheese. "There is one network that is bigger than Faceless, and far more intelligent."

"Don't tell me," said Jake, with a smile.

The Big Cheese ignored him. "And we mice will focus on this problem like a laser."

"So now what?" Jake asked.

"Now we wait," said the Big Cheese. "My security team will continue to watch Faceless, of course. But I am hoping for a shortcut. When they find that no new information is coming in, Faceless may well make a rash move, and be revealed."

It was almost dark now, and Megan was glad of the warmth of her mom next to her. Although she knew it was crazy, she couldn't help imagining people without faces sliding into this safe world. And she nearly screamed when the door burst open and a blurry figure stood there in the dim evening light.

But it was only Joey who'd just come from soccer practice in the rain, covered with mud, bringing everyone back to earth with his normal question of "What's for dinner?" He looked very surprised when his stepmother jumped up to give him a hug, in spite of the mud.

There was little rest at Headquarters that night. The Big Cheese had given the signal for "Code Six," an emergency code that was seldom used. It meant "all paws on deck." All two thousand adult mice, and a few of the teenagers, would have one mission: to track down the humans behind Faceless, especially those humans who were working with Loggocorp.

And yes, "all paws on deck" did indeed include the paws of camera mice and director mice and even performing mice. Until further notice, all work on the Megan Day Gala show would cease.

chapter four

hen Megan came home from school the next day she was glad to see her mom's car in the driveway. She'd had a hard time keeping faceless people out of her mind, and the thought of an empty house was not great.

"Any news?" she asked.

"Nothing," said her mom. "I feel so helpless, stuck over here."

"So why don't you go talk to Sir Brian yourself?" said Megan. "I'd have to come too, of course, because you promised, remember, when you went to that conference in Rome? That you'd take me along the next time you went to Europe?"

At least that made her mom laugh.

Megan did her homework in the kitchen that day, while Trey helped with algebra and Julia leaned comfortably against her neck. No way faceless people could slide under the door into this warm, bright room where her mom was thawing dinner because in her distracted state, she said, getting a meal ready from scratch wasn't going to happen.

The smell of meatloaf in the microwave was filling the kitchen when a bell rang in the corner, low down.

Megan sang out "Incoming!" and ran to the flap that closed off the mouse-tunnel, a long drainpipe that Uncle Fred had installed so that mice could run here from Planet Mouse with no danger from hawks or passing cats. The bell was a later addition, and a necessary one, because the first couple of times that a mouse skidded into view, Susie Fisher's reflexes acted faster than her scientific brain and she came out with some fearful EEEEKs, as if something about a mouse popping up at her feet pushed some deep evolutionary button. So Uncle Fred had set up a trigger inside the pipe that rang a warning bell when someone was about to appear.

This time, four mice shot into the room. First came a mouse with two dots on her ear—Julia—followed by her clan-mates Curly and Larry, their ears marked with one dot and three, respectively, so humans could tell them apart.

After them came Savannah. She didn't need dots, of course, because her hats did a much better job of identifying her. Today she'd chosen a big red one, its brim slightly bent from contact with the walls of the mouse-tunnel. And she was wearing a necklace that worked fine when she was sashaying on her hind legs—not so great when she had to run through a tunnel, and it kept getting tangled up with her front paws.

"It's not fair!" she said now, leaping onto the table to face Susie. "It's so not fair to me or my little Larrykins. Right, Larrykins?"

The humans were somewhat puzzled by the strong friend-ship that had grown between Larry and Savannah, because the two mice were absolute opposites. Larry was strong and silent (literally silent, since he hadn't been born with Talkmouth, the slightly floppy mouth that can be trained to make human sounds). Savannah was almost never silent, a mouse who loved the finer things in life—clothes, jewels, the glitter of Hollywood.

"What's not fair?" asked Susie, with only a ghost of the smile she usually wore when she was dealing with Savannah.

"My show!" wailed Savannah. "They've dropped my show! My gala! After all our work! I heard it was Sir Quentin's fault. That old . . . And my poor, poor Larrykins, his sports report all wasted!"

"Oh, come on," said Susie. "It's not that bad, is it? There'll be other galas!"

"But nothing like this! It was our big chance! My pathway to fame and fortune!"

Not for the first time, Megan marveled at the way Savannah could somehow forget she was a mouse. Fame? Yes, but only among mice. Fortune? No way she could make any money from the show, or spend money if she had it.

In his unhappiness, Larry had climbed up to the tabletop and was leaning against Megan's hand while Julia pressed herself against his other side to provide an all-over comfort wrap. But Megan could see from the way Larry gazed around the room that he really wanted Joey, wanted his boy. They had bonded because Joey was Larry's link to the sports he loved to follow, in the basketball season, the baseball season, and now the soccer season.

But where *was* Joey? Couldn't he somehow guess when he was needed? Couldn't he get his butt home once in a while, for his mouse?

It was almost dark. Jake had come home from Planet Mouse through the gate in the back fence and was setting the table when there was a clatter outside, the human equivalent of "incoming," the familiar sound of a bike being parked on its side.

Megan waited for Joey to burst into the kitchen, to sing out "Hi, Mom" to *her* mom, then to grab some crackers because his growth spurt couldn't wait for meatloaf.

But no. Instead, Megan heard the sound of a basketball. She ran to a window for a view of the driveway. Basketball *now*? In the *dark*? Then she saw why Joey hadn't come in, and she felt madder than ever. He'd actually invited a friend over. Someone who might even be coming in for a snack as Joey's seventh-grade friends often did, all of them growing, all of them able to eat a packet of cookies in one gulp.

"A Snuggle," Megan said as she turned back to the kitchen. "He's actually brought home a Snuggle."

Snuggle? Yes, that was the word that came out of one of the regular Tuesday meetings with the Big Cheese. Joey had referred to the humans who didn't Know as Muggles, which is what they'd be in Harry Potter's world, of course. The Big Cheese had tapped his mouth with his paw in the gesture that means "Laughing out loud."

"I see no necessity," he had said, while Sir Quentin translated his gestures, "to adapt a circumlocution previously tooled for humanoids of a fictional persuasion. It is surely prefer-able for the fertile brains of our inestimable band to develop a personalized nomenclature appropriate to our particular circumstances."

As he often did, Trey whispered a translation of the trans-lation. "Don't want to imitate Harry Potter. Better think of something that works for us."

And Snuggle was the name they chose, because (as Susie pointed out) it made the rest of humanity sound warm and cud-dly, which was fine because neither the five Humans Who Knew nor the Mouse Nation bore the rest of humanity any ill will.

Except right now. This was so not the time for a Snuggle invasion. With a Snuggle on the premises, the mice had to be ready to sprint for hiding places, or jump into the cage in the corner and follow the rules for WWAPMD, or "What Would a Pet Mouse Do"—taking turns on the exercise wheel while the Snuggle said, "Cool," or "EEEEK," or whatever.

Susie Fisher sighed. "Any way we can get rid of him?" she asked.

"I'll try," said Megan, and she headed outside.

This Snuggle didn't look like Joey's other friends, who were mostly jocks. This one was pale and pudgy with thick glasses, standing as if he had no clue what to do with the basketball in his hands. As he gave it a sort of little-kid heave that sent it about halfway to the rim, Joey turned to Megan, and his expression was unmistakable. "Help!"

Megan took the hint.

"Are you ever in trouble," she said, making herself scowl, which wasn't hard. "You're so late. Mom wants you inside—right now!"

"Okay," said Joey, and headed for the door. "Sorry, Ryan. Another time."

The boy reached out toward Joey as if he wanted to make him stay. Then he let his arms dangle, his face blank, before he turned to head out toward the street. That's when Megan saw the girl sitting cross-legged on the cold grass beside the driveway, shivering in a jacket that looked way too thin for this fall evening. She had the same pale look as the boy, as if she seldom went outside, and she looked vaguely familiar from school.

"Hi, Megan," said the girl. "Can you play?"

It wasn't hard to say, "Sorry, my mom needs me too," and to run back inside and shut the door, though not before she'd seen the man standing out in the street, watching.

"I was at Caden's house," Joey was explaining. "We're working on a project for social studies. This Ryan guy was waiting for me in the street, for some reason."

"He's a friend of yours?" asked Jake.

"No way, Dad! I don't think he has any friends. He said he

wanted a favor and he'd tell me about it when we got to my house. Weird."

"So what was the favor?" asked Jake.

"I dunno. He never told me," said Joey. "Hey, what's the problem? What's going on?"

Larry had rushed up his arm and settled on his shoulder, leaning against his neck. Mice can't cry, of course, but they do go into an all-over tremble when they're exceptionally sad, and now the mouse-vibrations were hard to ignore.

"I'll tell you what's going on," said Savannah. "I'll speak up for my poor Larrykins. Something happened with that rain forest or coconuts or something. Big deal. Well, okay, I know that's serious, but what's it got to do with galas? Tell me that!"

"Huh?" asked Joey.

"The Big Cheese stopped our gala! He said we might have to save it for next year! Next Megan Day! After all our work, me and Larrykins. We were both going to be famous and . . ."

"Hush, Savannah, hush," said Susie. "I'm sure it's just until the mice find those hackers. Megan Day's not for a couple of weeks, right? Maybe you'll get your show back."

There was a knock at the front door. It was Uncle Fred, though he usually came to The Fishery by way of the gate between the two backyards.

"I'd just locked up the office," he said. "I was heading back to my house when I ran into my old pal Jeff Crumline. He used to work with me at the computer shop, until they fired him because he was really bad with people. He wanted to know if we had any work for him."

"And you said no," said Jake.

"You kidding?" said Uncle Fred. "Course I said no."

"And?" asked Susie, who could tell when her brother was holding something back. "And, and, and?"

"He had his kids with him, Ryan and Emily. Said they'd like to come over and play. That was the word he used. Play."

"And you said?" prompted Jake.

"Well, I said it was up to Megan and Joey, obviously. Oh, and I told him you were both very busy. All the time," he added, with a grin at Megan.

It was a gift to Megan's mom, and here it came. Back to the topic Megan had been expecting yesterday, before the rain forest grabbed everyone's attention.

"Megan really isn't busy after school, are you, my love?" she said. "Emily might be very nice. And you could use some new friends. Right?"

"Mom, I don't *need* new friends!" said Megan. "I have plenty of friends."

Jake laughed.

"Maybe at least one of them should be human?" he said, reaching out to squeeze her shoulder.

When Megan came home from school the next day, Joey was doing homework in the kitchen, while Curly and Larry cruised for crumbs from the cookies he'd been eating.

"Any Snuggles follow you home?" she asked.

"Nope," he said, his mouth full of the peanut butter sandwich he was using to wash down the cookies.

She reached for the cookie packet, which was suspiciously light.

"You've finished them all? Again?"

"Left a couple for you," he said. "Or maybe just one."

"Grrr," said Megan. But at least having Joey in the kitchen gave her some protection against anything faceless that might try to sidle into The Fishery, so she took the cookie upstairs to her room, where Julia was waiting to give her the day's lesson in MSL.

Megan loved her lessons with Julia. She was brilliant at finding ways to adapt MSL for humans, so that braids and fingers made the signs normally assigned to ears and tails.

42

They'd reached a series of signs describing the weather, and Julia was demonstrating the rather violent gestures that mean "Thunderstorm" (it's the sign for rain—a pitter-pattering of paws—combined with sharp jumps) when Megan's phone rang. It was Uncle Fred, with the sort of bounce in his voice that meant people were listening at his end. His good old friend Jeff was at Planet Mouse, with his kids. Could she come over? And bring Joey?

So soon? Now? This was so much what Megan didn't want to do, for so many reasons. There was a scuttling under her dresser, and Trey appeared just as she clicked off the phone.

"You heard?" he said, a little out of breath. "I came over to warn you. Those are two strange kids."

"Do I have to go over?" she asked.

"By human rules, I guess you do," he said. "Besides, who knows?"

"You mean who knows if this might be my big chance for a real human friend?"

"That too," said Trey.

"What else? What do mice know about Emily?"

"Nothing," said Trey quickly. "If our guys have been checking up on her, I haven't heard about it."

It was something that mice often mentioned—the fact that

they had access to information about almost every human on the planet. It was a huge database made up of reports from hundreds of millions of mouse clans on their host families. A month ago, the five Humans Who Knew had asked the Big Cheese if they could have access to the database too. Wouldn't it be useful (for example) to know the truth about that strange guy Susie worked with at Cleveland State? Or about a big customer for solar belt-buckles who might not be able to pay? Or the teacher at Lakeview Middle School who seemed exceptionally mean?

"In our view," the Big Cheese had said, "access to such knowledge would be unhelpful. It would distort relationships that otherwise might prove fruitful and satisfying."

Trey was allowed to drop hints that helped Megan stay out of trouble with, say, an English teacher who hated rodents so much that she'd give a bad grade to any story involving mice. But he had heard nothing about Emily.

"Maybe she's what she seems," he said. "Maybe she just needs a friend."

Megan sighed, because did Emily's friend have to be *her*? She ran down to the kitchen to collect Joey, who was stuffing books into his backpack. "Good luck," he said. "I saw them arriving."

"So we both have to go over," she said.

"Dang! Wish I could, but I just remembered my soccer practice. Or band practice. Or chess club. Or something," said Joey. "Come on, guys."

He scooped up Larry and Curly and shot out of the house, leaving Megan to walk over to Planet Mouse by herself and pretend to be a normal kid, maybe even one who might be in need of a normal human friend.

chapter five

In the bright light of Planet Mouse, the three humans looked no less strange than they had last night. A skinny man, whose hair was even shaggier than Uncle Fred's. His son, peering through thick glasses, his T-shirt barely making it over his belly to his jeans. And the pale, skinny girl blinking behind the same sort of glasses as her brother.

They stood as if they were beings from another planet, unsure about the rules down here on Earth, not knowing whether they should sit, or stand, or smile, or hold out a hand in greeting.

Megan remembered the girl now. She'd noticed her at recess, always walking, keeping as far away from other kids as she could get. That had been Megan's own technique to get through recess in the many new schools that had been inflicted on her recently. Keep walking as if you're going somewhere.

But for a kid who wasn't new, who'd probably lived in this part of Cleveland for years, it was indeed weird. Or sad.

Over the top of the girl's head, Uncle Fred looked at Megan with what could have been an apology. "Sorry about this."

"Joey had to go off somewhere," Megan said.

"Okay," said Uncle Fred. "So Ryan can stay with us and take the tour while you and Emily hang out. Check?"

"Check," she said, giving Uncle Fred the look that means, "You owe me one," which he acknowledged with a sort of half smile.

Emily allowed herself to be led past the garage where seven hundred mice toiled secretly at the assembly lines of the mouse factory, and through the backyard to The Fishery.

"What would you like to do?" Megan asked, when they reached the kitchen.

For once she wished she'd done what her mom wanted—hung out with girls after school. Then at least she'd be more used to this. There hadn't been any girls her age on the island where she'd spent her third- and fourth-grade years, living in a cabin on the mountainside while her mom did research on wild sheep. When she came back to America—was it only last year?—she'd forgotten how to make friends with humans. It took months to get to know just one girl at her school in Oregon.

Caitlin. And Caitlin was the opposite of this . . . this lump of girl, this girl-shaped hole in the universe who followed Megan obediently without showing much interest in anything. Caitlin would be bubbling with ideas for things to do, like checking out Web sites, or playing basketball, or trying out a candy recipe.

But when Megan asked Emily, "What would you like to do?" all she got back was a shrug.

Megan was so not enjoying this. "Want to see my room?" she asked finally, dimly remembering what kids on television said in situations like this one.

"I guess," said Emily, in not much more than a whisper.

In Megan's room, Trey was nowhere to be seen. He must have gone underground, as he called it, lurking behind the walls or beneath furniture as he spied on human happenings. But Julia was on duty as pet mouse, dozing in the cage Megan had bought when Julia begged for her own exercise wheel.

The sight of Julia did seem to push a button in Emily, cranking her up to produce a few words.

"Can it do tricks on that computer?" she asked in a voice that was still almost a whisper, pointing at the Thumbtop on Megan's desk. "Your mouse?"

"Oh, you saw the show?" asked Megan.

Emily nodded because who hadn't seen the clips of Trey pretending to operate a Thumbtop on national television? That television show had been part of the Big Cheese's scheme to get Uncle Fred to New York, of course, part of the Nation's nice soft trap for him and Jake, luring them into a meeting with the Wall Street branch of the Mouse Nation to make a deal. But it had also meant instant fame.

"Let's see if he can remember those tricks," said Megan as she reached into the old cage, thinking how useful it was that it's almost impossible to tell male mice from females. Julia went into full WWAPMD, scrabbling around like a pet mouse to avoid the reaching hand, until she allowed herself to be cornered over by the exercise wheel.

Megan put her down next to the Thumbtop on her desk, her arms making a circle as if to keep a mouse from running away. After spinning around a couple of times in a display of her best WWAPMD, Julia turned to look blankly at the two girls as she backed up until she accidentally sat on the keyboard of the tiny computer. Then she turned and clicked on a couple of keys with her nose, to show that she could.

Megan laughed, but Emily didn't seem to do laughter. All she said was, "Can I try it?"

Megan thought fast. This was the Thumbtop her mice used, and she had no clue what it had been doing. Who'd been on it last? Was it Trey, chatting with old friends at the Talking Academy in San Francisco? Julia, e-mailing relatives from her original clan, the one in Uncle Fred's house? Had the last mouse signed off properly, leaving the Mouse Nation's site protected?

"Sorry," she said, crossing her fingers to cover the lie. "This Thumbtop has actually crashed—I'll have to get my uncle to fix it. You can try my laptop if you like. It's fairly new, and I'm still finding out what it can do."

She put the Thumbtop in her pocket and carried Julia back to the cage while Emily sat in front of the shiny new laptop on Megan's desk. Which was safe, wasn't it? The last thing Megan had done on it was to check out Creaturebook, the

social network site for endangered animals that the Humans
Who Knew had launched in partnership with Daisy Dakota,
who was probably the most famous teenage star on the planet.

Yes, Creaturebook. That was safe. Megan leaned over Emily's
shoulder and clicked to bring it up, navigating to the page that
showed Megan's own friend-animal, an endangered mouse
from an island just off the coast of Africa.

"See?" she explained. "You can click on your animal's
friends. Animals with the same sort of problem."

Emily obediently clicked and came to a picture of an endangered three-toed sloth. "This guy's in really bad shape," Megan
began, and pointed to the other "friends" on her mouse's page.
"Look, there's a flying squirrel from North Carolina and a
mountain beaver, and . . ." Her voice trailed off because Emily
wasn't looking at the Creaturebook page, but gazing up at
Megan with an expression that seemed to mean, "Why are you
hovering like that?"

To be polite, Megan backed away. But as she did so, she
made a sign to Julia in the cage. It was a sign Julia had taught
Megan only last week—the right paw (or hand) touching the
forehead just above the right eye. "Keep watch."

Megan picked up a book and sat on her bed, pretending
not to be suspicious, pretending to read for all of three minutes

before she felt a slight tug on the bedspread that meant a mouse was climbing up. Trey.

He squirmed up to her ear and whispered, "Come with me. Big bedroom."

"Be right back," she said, but Emily barely looked up as Megan carried Trey out to her parents' bedroom, the one that overlooked the backyard, and beyond it the yard at Planet Mouse, and the three-car garage that housed the factory.

There was Ryan, trundling a garbage can over toward the factory's high window. They watched as he clambered onto the can so he could peer through the window where he'd see . . . well, absolutely nothing, because Jake had blocked off the view, just in case.

Originally, Jake had covered the window completely, but the worker mice complained—politely, which is the way of mice. They had loved the glimpse of leaves and sky that had come through that window. So Jake compromised, putting up just enough of a baffle to block human eyes while leaving a bit of view for the mice inside.

"Do you think he has a clue what's in there?" Megan whispered anxiously. "Do you think he can hear the machinery?"

"Hope not," said Trey. "But I'll tell Mr. Fred to get him out of there, just in case." He hopped off Megan's shoulder and sprinted downstairs for the mouse-tunnel.

Megan stayed at the window of the master bedroom until Trey must have arrived at Planet Mouse, because she saw Uncle Fred saunter out, with Emily's dad in tow. They couldn't miss Ryan, still perched on his garbage can.

Megan saw Uncle Fred laugh, then wave at the side door of the garage as if inviting both Jeff and his son to take a look. And he unlocked the door to display—well, nothing. Nothing but a wall of cardboard boxes all stamped THUMBTOPS FOR DELIVERY. Just a warehouse full of computers that could have been made in China. Or Malaysia. Maybe Ecuador. Wherever.

Of course Uncle Fred wouldn't have shown them the secret button on the wall that caused a column of boxes to swing inward, revealing what went on behind them: seven hundred mice busy on the assembly lines.

"Sorry I took so long," lied Megan, getting back to her room. "I thought I heard someone at the front door. And then, of all things—"

But Emily didn't look as if she'd missed her. All her attention was on the computer. Megan glanced at the screen and felt as if little electric shocks were sprinting up and down her body. Emily was looking at a report about the effects of melting icebergs on the currents of the North Atlantic—a site Megan's mom had urged her to check out, what, two days ago? Three? Was Emily working her way backward through Megan's whole history, all the sites she had looked at recently? Might she find one that hinted at the evolution of mice? Hinted at the truth?

A movement in the cage caught Megan's eye. Julia was frantically making the sign for "End it," the paw drawn quickly across the throat. But how? Should Megan just grab the computer? Knock Emily off her chair? Make up some lie? How did people handle this sort of situation?

Through luck, as it turned out. The luck of having Susie Fisher come home at just the right moment, so Megan could say, "Hey, let's go downstairs and you can meet my mom."

Emily closed the laptop and the danger was over.

chapter six

The two girls sat in the kitchen at The Fishery for about twenty minutes while Susie tried to keep a conversation going, asking Emily about school (okay) and her brother (sometimes a jerk) and her dad (working on some great apps that he hoped he could sell).

True, Susie's first instinct (as she told Megan later) was to give the girls cookies and send them off to bond. But Megan's plea was unmistakable: the MSL sign for "Help." (It's the tail, or a braid, held straight up.)

After Jeff Crumline finally rang the front doorbell to collect his kid, Megan told her mom what had happened. She had just begun to describe Emily's search through her computer when Uncle Fred arrived, puffing from his quick run through the backyards. He told Susie about Ryan's attempts to peer into the garage.

"So both kids were *spying*?" squeaked Susie. She sat down, hard.

"Looks like it," said Uncle Fred. "Spying and maybe getting ready for some hacking. Jeff knows how to hack, that's for sure. When he was working at the computer shop, he used to boast about how he could get into *any* system. Like newspaper offices. Big banks. Said he was teaching Ryan and it had paid off, because how else could he get that A in history? Can you imagine? Proud of his kid for hacking into the school computers?"

"So close to home," said Susie, in a small voice. "Hackers. Do you think your Jeff is connected with Faceless? Is that what's going on?"

"Could be," said Uncle Fred, his face grim.

"Do you think they've guessed something about mice?" asked Megan. "Or just rain forests?"

"Not about mice," said Uncle Fred. "When Jeff asked where the Thumbtops are made, I said they are assembled by mice, just like it says on our sign. He laughed, or came as close to laughing as he ever does. Didn't believe it for a second."

Which left the rain forest.

There had to be a meeting with the Big Cheese, of course, and it began like none other, with an apology. Well, maybe it wasn't a full-throated apology, but at least his signs looked a little humble as he faced the humans.

"I am sorry that some of you spent a difficult afternoon," he began, but he had to stop because Megan's mom was determined to have her say.

"Surely we should have been warned," she said. "I mean, you have this database you're so proud of, but you let Megan entertain someone who hunted through her computer. You let that boy run loose all over Planet Mouse."

It's hard for a mammal whose speech is silent to interrupt, but the Big Cheese found a way, grasping the open door of the cage and banging it back against the bars.

"Your afternoon may have been uncomfortable," he said, his eyes fixed unblinking on Susie, "but it was extremely useful to us. As I said two days ago, it was my hope that we could drive your enemies into the open. And it appears that we were successful."

"But you didn't even raise a paw to warn us!" said Susie.

The Big Cheese ignored her. "We suspect that the adult male and the immature male are allied with Faceless," he said. "But we cannot be sure. There is an excellent reason for our uncertainty. Our database on humans is, alas, incomplete. It cannot include households that are infested."

"Cat there, huh?" said Uncle Fred. "At the Crumlines'?"

"A veritable herd of cats," said the Big Cheese with a shudder. "According to the clan in a neighboring house, there are more than a half dozen, and two of them are pregnant, so the situation will only become worse."

"So what do you suggest?" asked Jake. "Should we play along with the Crumlines? See where that leads us?"

"An excellent word choice, if I may say so," said the Big Cheese. "Because I propose that one of you should continue to 'play along.' Our first step should be to arrange another of those occasions that you humans call 'playdates.'"

"You don't mean—" Megan began. "Oh please! Sir!"

The Big Cheese looked right at her now. "I understand that your afternoon with the young female was not to your liking," he said. "But given the excess of cats at the Crumline residence, our only hope for access is through human intervention."

"You mean Megan goes in as a *spy*?" asked Joey.

"Not exactly," said the Big Cheese. "Mice will do the spying. Miss Megan will provide transportation, leaving a couple of our operatives in the house. It will be a slam dunk, as you humans say."

"But it's not that easy," squeaked Megan. "It's not like we're friends. Not like we'll *ever* be friends. Couldn't Joey—"

"I'd do it," said Joey, "but you know Emily better than I know Ryan."

"He's right," said her mom. "And hey, look on the bright side. It will be good for you. Good practice in social skills."

And that's how Megan found herself calling Emily that night after dinner, under the eyes of the other four Humans Who Knew, with her fingers crossed to cover her lies.

"That was fun today," the other humans heard. "Want to hang out tomorrow, after school? Yes, your place would be great. See ya."

When she put the phone down, Megan noticed that Joey was grinning at her and clapping his hands silently.

"What?" she asked.

"Just—just, you did good."

"Huh?"

He looked exasperated. "Can't you take a compliment?"

"Sorry," she said. "Thanks. But the next time—"

"Of course," he said. "Next time it's my turn."

Megan smiled, but inside she felt a bit of a secret "Grrr." As well as being better than her at almost everything else, was Joey now better at being *nice*?

Emily was waiting after school as Megan unlocked her bike, and they walked more or less in silence the five blocks to Emily's house. There was an old truck parked on what had once been grass, and the house had brown patches showing through its dirty white paint. A rusty basketball hoop clung to the eaves of the garage.

This kept on happening to Megan. Ever since she'd met mice, she'd found herself going into buildings that made her nervous. Like the time Trey had led her into Headquarters in Silicon Valley—or worse, that empty house they'd broken into in Oregon to use its webcam.

This time at least her adults knew where she was and could send out a search party if necessary. And hey, this was just a good old-fashioned playdate, right? If you had playdates in sixth grade. The fact that Emily was weird didn't mean she was dangerous. Did it?

She wished Trey had come with her, but he really, really didn't want to, and she couldn't blame him. How many cats were there in the house? Seven? Eight? Yes, he'd be safe in her pocket, or tucked into the backpack, but as Megan knew, the smell of even one cat is enough to make a mouse feel sick.

"Besides, you'll already have two guys in the caboose," he'd said. "Not much room for more."

The caboose. That's what he called the pocket of her backpack, where he often rode to school, peering out through the pinhole she'd punched through the fabric. And true, the caboose was bulging now with two mice from the IT department and their supplies. They'd been chosen, Trey had told her, not just for their great eyesight but for their bravery. These guys didn't tremble. And nothing would have given the mission away more quickly than a trembling backpack.

Megan was glad to see that Emily let herself into the house, because the fewer Crumlines who were around, the better. Fewer cats would have been better too: at least five ran toward Emily purring and rubbing against her legs.

Normally if you take a backpack full of mice into the neighborhood of a cat, the cat will leap for it. To short-circuit this response, Susie had gone online to find a list of herbs that can block other smells and had made an herbal sachet from one of Jake's old handkerchiefs.

True, a couple of the cats seemed to sniff the air, but only, it seemed, out of mild curiosity, not from bloodlust. So Megan felt it was safe to leave her backpack on a table near the front door.

Emily led her to the kitchen and picked up a stack of dirty plates from the table. The sink was full already, so she pushed some empty pizza boxes along the counter to clear a space for the plates, then turned to look at Megan.

"Sorry about the mess," she said.

"That's okay," said Megan. "You should see my uncle's place."

Then Emily did the worst thing she could have done. She grinned at Megan, and said, "Yeah, those nerds."

Megan couldn't help grinning back, as if this girl was all right, which was not the way it should happen. Why couldn't Emily have kept up that weird sort of distance so Megan could have disliked her? So she could have gotten on with her job without any second thoughts—the job of spying on Emily's family.

Emily was still grinning.

"This is so cool," she said. "Like yesterday I was mad at my dad for saying, you know, that I wanted to hang out with you, because I didn't. Well, I did, but I never said that, and I could tell that you . . . well, I thought that you . . ."

Her voice trailed off, and Megan heard herself say, "I was a bit mad at my uncle too for setting it up without asking, but hey, it's good to have someone to hang out with."

She kept her fingers crossed as she'd said it, because she didn't mean it was good, at least not yet, though actually hanging out with Emily turned out to be not too bad after all. Better than yesterday, certainly. As they ate leftover pizza, Emily asked a lot of questions, and Megan found that she liked telling her about her mom's research into the effect of climate change on animals, and what it was like spending a couple of years on a remote island in the Atlantic, and how glad she was, basically, that her mom had got married again, because Jake was the coolest stepdad you could hope for.

By the time they finished eating, Megan was beginning to feel that she knew Emily well enough to ask *her* some questions. To do some research, though she approached it sideways.

"You seem really interested in computers," she said. "Like when you were looking at mine."

Emily laughed. "Sorry about that," she said. "It must have seemed a bit weird. My dad asked me to see what sort of sites you'd been looking at. He says it helps him design games, knowing what kids do on their computers. They're great, some of his games. There's one he's just finished that's really cool. Come on, I'll show you."

Emily led the way into her bedroom.

"Here's the game," she said, sitting down at a desk made of an old door. "It's called Hackety-Hack."

"It's called *what*?" squeaked Megan.

Emily laughed. "It's a hacking game. Watch. You pretend you're hacking into the White House. Or the Pentagon. See, I'll show you."

She made some clicks on her computer and worked her way

past pages labeled Top Secret and Classified and War Room, a slight smile on her face, and yes, the game did look cool.

"Your dad's really good," said Megan.

Emily sighed. "Yeah, but he can't seem to sell anything." She reached for a flash drive and stuck it in her computer. "He said it would be so great if you could show it to your uncle. Maybe he can help my dad to, you know, get someone interested? Do you mind?"

Megan felt chills like little mouse feet running up and down her spine. Here it came, the dropping of the other shoe. Jeff Crumline's attack. Faceless at work. Whatever. A game that was hard to resist, a game that was designed to suck the brains out of Uncle Fred's computer, then Jake's computer, and her mom's, and from there to the computers of every rain forest expert in the world. An attack on all Loggocorp's enemies in one go.

It didn't take long for Emily to copy the game onto the flash drive and hand it over.

"You can give the flash drive back tomorrow," she said.

Right. When it would be too late for some computers at least. When the damage had been done.

Megan forced herself to smile and say, "Thanks" as she took the tiny flash drive and put it in her pocket. Then she watched as Emily seemed to sigh with relief, like a kid who'd finished a job for her dad and could get back to her own life.

"Want to play a video game?" she asked, pointing to a console in the corner. "I've got a new one about a girl detective. It's really cool."

"In a minute," said Megan. "I need to use the bathroom."

"It's down the hall," said Emily. "I'll show you."

"I saw it," said Megan. "Be right back."

Out in the hallway, she opened the door to the bathroom, then closed it again from the outside. Then she grabbed her backpack from the table near the front door and hurried into a room she'd glimpsed when they came into the house, a room full of computers. She moved aside a couple of the books that were loosely stacked on the shelves that covered one wall and lifted up the cargo from the caboose, piece by piece: two mice, one ball of herbs, one empty plastic bag for poop, one full bag of cheese crackers, and a Thumbtop that had been wiped clean of almost everything except its camera.

"Can those mice send a message, at least?" Megan had asked.

"Sure," said Uncle Fred. "When they're ready to be picked up."

"What if the Crumlines find them before that?" asked Megan.

"Then they'd have to push the Doomsday button," he said.

Ah yes, the Doomsday button. Every Thumbtop in the field had one so that if by chance a mouse clan knew their Thumbtop was about to fall into the hands of Snuggles, they could send a last urgent message to Headquarters. Then they'd kill the computer with one click, leaving nothing for the humans to find but an empty case with no brain.

"Bye, guys," whispered Megan. "Good luck. We'll get you out in a couple of days."

chapter seven

'm proud of you," said Susie Fisher, grinning for the first time in days.

She was sitting in the kitchen when Megan came back from Planet Mouse, where she'd left the little flash drive at the top of the stairs for the IT mice to study.

"I'm not proud of me," said Megan. "It's not Emily's fault that her dad's such a creep."

"So maybe you two really can be friends!" said her mom. "When all this is over."

Megan gave her The Look. That famous mouse look, that silent, chilling glare that can freeze certain mammals in their tracks. And it sort of worked.

"Okay, okay," said her mom. "It's your life. Right?"

And that life wasn't too easy for Megan the next day, because Emily acted as though they could really be friends, as if everything that happened at her house was normal, as if that little flash drive really did hold only a cool game. When there was no way, right? It must be awash with viruses, stuffed with secret commands.

Maybe Emily didn't *know* what her dad was up to? Because she asked Megan if they could hang out after school again today.

Luckily it really was Megan's day for mousekeeping at the factory, filling the food bowls and emptying the poop. So she could honestly say she was busy without the risk of going red, which happened all too often when she had to lie.

Emily's smile vanished so fast that Megan felt guilty enough to say, "How about next Tuesday?"

The grin on Emily's face was embarrassing. Nobody should be so needy.

Normally the report on the flash drive would have been sent to the humans by e-mail, but all e-mails between mice and humans had stopped until further notice, for reasons of security. So it was a messenger mouse who rang the Incoming bell that night with a Thumbtop strapped to his back.

Susie peered at the screen of the Thumbtop through the magnifying glass that she wore around her neck.

"Oh no!" she exclaimed. Then laughed, because what she read out was:

> **Flash drive is clean except for good game (now on our Web site for general mouse use).**

"What!" exclaimed Megan, as her worldview—and in particular her Emily-view—readjusted itself, and she went a bit red. "So when Emily was searching through my computer—"

"Probably just wanted to find out what girls like you are interested in, like she told you," said her mom, with a slightly smug smile. "When are you seeing her again?"

"Tuesday," said Megan in a small voice.

But Tuesday never happened. At least not in this hemisphere.

It was early the next afternoon that the mice on the Crumlines' bookshelf sent out their signal. Mayday, mayday. Help. The herb smell must be wearing off, because the cats had started to look up at the bookshelf in a way that might make the humans suspicious.

This time it was Joey's turn, which is why at about four o'clock he just happened to be pedaling past the Crumlines' house with his basketball under one arm when he spotted the antique hoop that Megan had described, clinging to the eaves.

And when he just happened to feel the need to use that hoop, the sound of his bouncing ball brought out Ryan, blinking in surprise. Of course he joined in, in his clunky little-kid way, but Joey did almost all the running around, which meant he got all sweaty. Then it was the most natural thing in the world to ask for a drink of water, and go into the house for it, and while he was there to wander into the room full of computers, saying, "Man, your dad really has some cool stuff." It was perfectly natural too to stand with his back to the bookshelf so that two mice and a Thumbtop and two plastic bags and a bundle of herbs could tumble gratefully into the hood of his sweatshirt.

Back at Planet Mouse, Joey ran up the stairs and sat down on the fourth stair from the top, leaning back so the mice could unload themselves from his hood, and hand over the precious Thumbtop to the IT team that was waiting for it.

It was after dinner at The Fishery. Everyone was a little tense, waiting for word from Headquarters—word about Jeff Crumline and what really went on in his computer room.

Megan was loading the dishwasher while mice cruised the tabletop for crumbs from the apple pie that her mom had bought from a store, because with all this tension, neither she nor Jake felt like cooking.

Savannah had decided to spend the evening with her humans. As she put it, "I don't want to be anywhere near the Big Cheese right now, not after what he did to me and my poor Larrykins. If I saw him I might just *puke!*" (which was safe to say because puking is something mice can't actually do).

Sir Quentin too had taken refuge in The Fishery as he nursed his disappointments over the canceled gala. It was beneath his dignity to hunt for crumbs, so he was sitting on a countertop reading an old copy of Shakespeare's plays that Jake had saved from college.

Was the bell for incoming unusually loud? Certainly all the humans jumped and ran to the corner of the room as Trey shot out of the tunnel. They were summoned. Immediately. Megan couldn't get any more out of him as he rode on her shoulder over to Planet Mouse.

It was Joey who ran up the stairs to collect the old birdcage, which was bulging with mice because the Big Cheese had ordered three of his directors to ride with him. He introduced the Director of Information Technology, as you'd expect.

The Director of Security—also no surprise. But the Director of Transportation?

"May we ask who is to be transported where?" asked Jake, when the Big Cheese had made the introductions.

"All in good time," said the Big Cheese, as Trey translated. "Stay tuned. First, let us share the photographs of the Crumline computer, the screenshots, if you will. Here."

He pushed a Thumbtop toward the door of the cage. Uncle Fred connected it to the monitor in the corner of the office so the screenshots would be big enough for humans to see.

To Megan it didn't make much sense at first: pages of computer code that could all have been games, as far as she knew. But then came e-mails. E-mails about listening devices. E-mails about rain forests. E-mails from Loggocorp. The smoking gun.

"These e-mails give us ample evidence of Mr. Crumline's involvement in Faceless, and evidence also that his son was assisting him," said the Big Cheese. "However," he added, with a look in Megan's direction, "Miss Megan will be glad to hear that the young female knew nothing of this. Indeed, our operatives report that the father made it very clear to the son that the girl-child must be kept in ignorance."

According to one e-mail, someone was profoundly disappointed that Jeff Crumline had failed to find out through that Fisher woman what exactly Sir Brian was planning with regard to the Marisco rain forest. Loggocorp would have to redouble its efforts to get information about Sir Brian's plans the old-fashioned way—by hiring humans in Great Britain to follow his group, starting at the hotel near the airport where they had arranged to assemble.

"As you know, Sir Brian has arranged for trusted students to meet the rain forest experts at the airport and drive them to a certain hotel," said the Big Cheese. "That hotel may now be compromised, so the British branch of the Mouse Nation has made reservations at a different one. From there the experts will be driven to the location where they will meet Coconut Man's descendant, as originally planned."

"Great," said Susie, reaching out to Uncle Fred to borrow his phone. "If you give me the name of that new hotel, I'll get a message to . . ."

"Put away the phone," said the Big Cheese, with the sign for a slight smile. "We have a better solution. One as old as time. We suggest that you should tell Sir Brian in person."

"What, me?" said Susie. "Go to London?"

"Why not?" said the Big Cheese. "It is my belief that your presence there will be immensely valuable, both for your contributions to Sir Brian's group and as a liaison with the British branch of the Mouse Nation. Because it is they, of course, who will introduce the group to the descendant of Coconut Man. A person who can make decisions for the whole family. To allay suspicion, we will also purchase a ticket for you, Mr. Jake. You can let it be known that this is what humans call a second honeymoon."

"Sounds good to me," said Jake, with a huge grin. "Fred, you can move into our house for a few days, right? Keep an eye on the kids?"

"Not this kid," said Joey.

"Huh?" said Jake and Susie together.

"Remember, Dad? When you went to that trade show in Paris last year? You absolutely promised I could come the next time."

Megan laughed. "And Mom definitely promised that the next time she goes to Europe, I'm coming too."

Susie Fisher put her head in her hands for a moment, but when she looked up she was grinning.

"When do we go?" she asked.

Thanks to the Transportation Department and the Mouse Nation's credit card (in Uncle Fred's name), the humans didn't have to bother with details like booking plane tickets and rental cars. That left time for them to dig out their suitcases and find their passports and clean socks. And it left time for Lakeview Middle School to give its permission, and for teachers to set up homework assignments.

Even in the bustle of getting ready, you couldn't miss what was going on with the mice, who would all have to be left behind. It was Britain's fault, because of its strict laws to keep the disease of rabies out of their country. As the mice knew, if a dog or a cat sets one paw on British soil it is whisked

off to quarantine for months unless it has a special passport. And pet mice? Forget about it. No way a mouse can get into Britain unless he (or she) is part of a batch headed straight for a research laboratory.

Julia was looking particularly sad. Ever since she and Megan had met just over a year ago, they'd hardly ever been apart. When the humans had a final meeting with the Big Cheese, Julia was crouched on Megan's right shoulder leaning against her neck in the comfort position. Trey was in the comfort position on her left shoulder, and Sir Quentin, who was interpreting for the Big Cheese, drooped.

"You will be provided with an interpreter who will enable you to communicate with British mice," the Big Cheese said. "Talking Mouse Ten will join you at London Airport."

Though that's not the way it came out from Sir Quentin. Something about a designated representative of the murine population of that sceptered isle, spoken in a voice almost too soft and sad and envious for them to hear.

While the humans were doing their final packing, the Big Cheese felt more serene than he had for days. His security team and his IT team would continue to work on the rain forest case, of course, to keep his humans and their secrets safe. But the

need for "all paws on deck" was over, which was good because ever since he'd postponed the Megan Day show, morale around Headquarters had taken a hit.

"The Youth Chorus is acting up," the Director of Media told his boss. "It's hard for the Master of Mouse Music to control them. One of the Mousettes ate her pom-pom. And Talking Mouse Seven, Savannah. Remember what Victorian heroines used to do?"

The Big Cheese thought back to the course on Human Literature that all mice take online. "They swooned?" he suggested. "Got the vapors?"

"Vapors is about right," said the director. "She's on the set, lying on the couch, looking as if her world has ended. Oh, and Cleveland Mouse 42, the one they call Larry, is lying on the ground beside her. Could be dead, if you didn't know better."

The Big Cheese smiled. "Since our humans will now be in charge of their own destiny," he said, "we can spare enough mouse power to proceed with the show. Please spread the word that rehearsals will start anew. We still have time before Megan Day."

Savannah leapt off her couch, Larry sort of reinflated himself, and Curly along with him. They rushed through the pipe-tunnel to The Fishery with the news that at least the mice who were taking part in the gala show were happy.

chapter eight

The humans were gathered in the kitchen of The Fishery, in the chaos of departure. Curly, Larry, and Savannah had said their good-byes and sprinted back to Headquarters for rehearsals. But Sir Quentin, Trey, and Julia were lined up on the kitchen table, all with the droop to their whiskers that you'd expect. The droop of mice about to be abandoned.

"Maybe we could smuggle them into England," said Joey.

"Are you kidding?" said Susie. "Do you know what would happen if we were caught? The British are so strict about animals coming in! The mice would probably be killed. And we might go to jail."

So it was good-bye. When Uncle Fred drove up, ready to take the humans to the airport, Megan gave Sir Quentin a soothing scratch behind the ears and lifted Julia up for a good-bye nuzzle, nose to nose.

Then Trey.

But Trey didn't want the usual nose-to-nose farewell. Instead he whispered, "Ear," and when Megan put him on her shoulder he whispered something that was not good-bye at all. Something more like, "See ya."

"What? What? What?" Megan whispered, but Trey had wriggled free. She looked around to see if there were any more clues. Any changed expressions on a mouse? No, all three were apparently still sunk in gloom. But could that be a wink from Uncle Fred? And once everyone was in his car, what did it mean when he dashed back into the house for a shopping bag, saying he'd be doing his marketing on the way home, even though the bag looked as if it had something inside it already?

As Uncle Fred gave Megan a last hug at the airport, he whispered instructions. In forty-five minutes precisely, she should put her backpack down in the corner of a certain gift shop, next to the pile of newspapers.

It didn't take long to go through security. Plenty of time for Megan to saunter into the gift shop and put her backpack down for a moment beside the pile of newspapers in the corner. She stood as close to the backpack as possible, trailing her jacket over it so no one would see the shapes darting out from behind the newspapers—one of them dragging an empty plastic bag—and into the caboose that was conveniently open.

After that, in the short night over the Atlantic Ocean, Megan saw nothing of mice, felt nothing, heard nothing except for some brief whispers as they flew into the dawn, a voice in her ear that told her what should happen after they landed.

If there's one thing that helps cope with jet lag it's the knowledge that your backpack is illegal and that you'll have only a few seconds to fix it.

This time it wasn't a gift shop that Megan had to look for. There weren't any in this part of London Airport: just endless corridors, one much like the other. At last Megan saw what she'd been told to expect, a huge poster proclaiming that London was the capital of the world, with a small construction site just beyond it. It was there that weary passengers trooping toward the immigration hall saw an eleven-year-old girl put her heavy backpack down for a minute and pull a jacket out of it, taking just a little longer than she needed.

Then all Megan had to do was to throw the plastic bag from the caboose into the trash. No point trying to explain mouse poop to the customs guys.

. . . .

As the humans passed through immigration and waited for their bags, Megan started to get nervous. Not about the customs guys, but about her parents. How would they feel about the risk she'd taken, smuggling mice into England? The risk that their friends might be caught, and exterminated?

After they picked up their rental car, Jake drove around to a loading bay behind the terminal—the spot where Talking Mouse Ten would be waiting for them. Right on cue, a mouse ran out toward them. Then another. Then another.

"Look!" said Susie. "They've sent us a whole welcoming committee!"

Megan made a quick count. Four. One must be Trey. But who else? She couldn't see from here, and sank down in her seat, hoping to be invisible enough to avoid what was coming.

Susie opened her window, which was about level with the loading bay, and mice streamed over the back of her seat and down into the two cupholders between the front seats.

"Mornin', all," said one, sticking out his head. "How you doin'? Me name's Ken, and I hope you don't mind but I've brought along some of me China plates."

"China plates?" asked Susie weakly.

"China plates meaning mates, right?" said Jake, who'd once worked in London for six months. "Friends. That Cockney rhyming slang—I thought it had died out."

"Well, maybe it has for humans, yeah?" said Ken. "Up to us mice to keep up the old ways, innit."

"Indeed," came a lugubrious voice from the bottom of a cupholder. "Kenneth chooses to perpetuate an outmoded dialect that originated, if I may say so without causing offense, in the working classes."

Susie grinned.

"Forgive me," she said, "but you sound just like a friend of ours, an American talking mouse."

"Interesting," said the mouse. "And I had thought myself to be unique in the murine world." Then his voice sank into a sort of "flumph" as if (to Megan's relief) someone, some mouse, was holding his mouth shut. And she hoped it would stay shut at least until Jake was used to driving on the left and could find a quiet spot to pull over. Because surely he'd freak out when he learned the truth. And her mom . . .

Megan pretended to be asleep, hoping the situation would go away. Except that it couldn't, could it, especially when one part of the problem was wriggling out of its cupholder and making its way to the back of Susie's seat.

When Susie came out with an "EEEEK," because her mouse tolerance must have been weakened by jet lag or something, the mouse in question said, "Forgive me, madam, but as one who has waited his whole life for the opportunity to visit this country, I was overwhelmed by an inexorable craving for my first view of this blessed isle."

Now there was no way. No way anyone could have had any doubts. Jake nearly put the car under a bus as he drove through a roundabout, one of the traffic circles that English drivers roar around with great confidence, but Americans fresh off the plane—not so much. Jake totally missed his exit and was trapped on the inside of the roundabout for two more circuits until he managed to get off into the quietest available exit. He pulled over and put his head down on the steering wheel.

"Bit of a shock, innit," said Ken. "That's why I told you these geezers was locals, like from my clan. Just until you was more settled. But that wasn't going to work, was it? Not with Sir Talkative here."

No, it wasn't going to work. Not when Sir Quentin hadn't

been able to overcome his need for a clear view of what he called his spiritual home. Not when the other two mice who now emerged were so distinctive: Trey with a piece missing from his right ear where a rat had chomped it long ago, and Julia with the two marker dots on her left.

Susie turned to the back seat.

"Who was it?" she asked icily. "Which of you did this? You knew the risk. You knew the mice would probably be killed if anyone found them in your luggage. And *we'd* have been in deep trouble. Maybe our whole mission. How *could* you? . . ."

"We were in Megan's backpack, but please don't blame her!" said Trey. "It was our idea. And Mr. Fred's. He dropped us off at the airport and told Megan where to find us."

Susie put her head in her hands, and Trey kept talking to fill the silence. Burbling, really, about how Savannah and Larry wanted to stay home to work on the show, and Curly too. How Sir Quentin had recorded his ode yesterday, so he was free to come. And yes, it was a risk. But missing an adventure like this? Not going to happen.

More silence, then it was Ken who spoke. "The more the merrier, yeah?"

Jake reached over and patted his wife's knee.

"Hey, now that they're all here, I think we should take advantage. Like get someone to interpret Ken."

"Now then, what are you talkin' about?" said Ken. "Are you sayin' I don't talk proper? It's not like I'll be rhymin' all the time. Just for a bit of a laugh, yeah?"

"A laugh," said Sir Quentin. "Hilarious."

To Megan's huge relief, her mom smiled as she reached out to tickle him behind the ears.

chapter nine

he plan called for the four humans to spend a couple of days in London before they joined the rain forest experts. British mice had booked them into an apartment on the south bank of the River Thames. And what an apartment! It blew everybody's mind. The living room seemed to dangle right over the river, with a perfect view of the Houses of Parliament on the other bank. If it was too much for the humans, it was way, way, way too much for Sir Quentin, tripping a circuit in his brain that brought on an explosion of poetry.

He ran to the windowsill and gazed across the river as he intoned:

> This royal throne of kings, this scepter'd isle,
> This earth of majesty, this seat of Mars . . .

"Yeah, yeah, yeah," said Ken, climbing out of Jake's pocket, where he'd been riding. "Lovely stuff. 'This blessed plot, this earth, this realm, this England.' We all had to learn it. Shakespeare, innit? *Richard the Second*. But now we got a job to do. Right? Take a message to that Sir Brian about where them experts should be delivered, from the airport."

"And his place is near here, isn't it?" said Jake.

"That's right, governor, so no worries. We can be there in a tick. It's an easy walk. Piece of chalk. I'll show you."

Using Jake's Thumbtop, Ken pulled up the satellite view of their building, then panned over to an apartment building only three blocks away.

"That's why we picked this flat," he said. "That and the view, for his lordship there."

He pointed at Sir Quentin, still rapturously glued to his view of the Thames and the Houses of Parliament.

"I'll go over to Sir Brian's now," said Susie.

"I'm comin' with you, if I may be so bold," said Ken. "I'll talk to that there clan at Sir Brian's. Get our strategy straight."

"I'm coming too," said Jake. "Just in case. You kids can hang here, okay? Check out the TV, or take a nap."

. . . .

It was so quiet after the adults had gone. Dead quiet, except for the whispered poetry from the windowsill where Sir Quentin had switched from Shakespeare to Wordsworth, and in particular the poem he wrote on Westminster Bridge:

> *Earth has not anything to show more fair*
> *Dull would he be of soul who could pass by*
> *A sight so touching in its majesty...*

"If I sit down," announced Megan, flopping on the couch, "I may never get up."

It was, after all, six in the morning in Cleveland, which meant that the midday sunlight out there looked fake. Had it been like this the last time she'd flown to Europe? When her mom took her to the Atlantic island where they spent two years doing research on wild sheep?

Yes, she remembered something of this feeling, when nothing seems quite real, as if you've fallen through a gap in the universe into a different dimension of time and space. Yes, a nap would be good.

For Joey there was something more urgent than sleep.

"Let's see if there's anything here to eat," he said. Megan hauled herself off the couch to follow him into the spotless kitchen, with Trey and Julia on her shoulders. It did not look promising. Nothing in the little refrigerator. And in the cabinets, nothing but a small jar labeled "Marmite" and a container of something called Fru-Grains.

"Looks like mouse food but bigger," said Trey when Joey opened it up. "Maybe rat food."

Joey held out a handful of chunks and Trey took an experimental nibble. "It's sweet," he said. "Won't kill you. Humans probably put milk on it. Or that stuff."

He pointed to the jar of Marmite. Megan found a teaspoon and dug some out for Trey, who took a small lick of it and then rushed to the paper towel dispenser to wipe it off his tongue.

"Barf," he said. "That stuff is bad. It's just wrong."

So the choice was simple. Either dry Fru-Grains/rat food with or without Marmite, or wait until the adults came back. Or?

"We passed a McDonald's, remember?" said Joey. "About a block from here."

"You think it's okay to go out?" asked Megan.

"Well, either that or we starve to death," said Joey. "And look." He burrowed into his backpack and brought out an envelope full of money. "Dad kept these pounds from the last time he was here."

They looked at each other. No one had told them they had to stay here and starve. And in a few minutes they'd found the way to cope with jet lag. You go to a McDonald's and your body can believe it is still in Cleveland as you eat the familiar burgers and fries and pass bits of familiar bun to pockets carrying very familiar mice.

Only Sir Quentin remained in the apartment, riveted by his view.

When Joey was finally full, after two of everything, they sauntered back toward the flat. They decided to take the long way round along a busy riverside walkway so they could feel fully abroad. It had rained while they were eating, but now the sun was lighting up the Houses of Parliament on the other bank of the river and the clock tower of Big Ben.

They stopped for a while to watch the boats on the river, and it was a lucky choice, to dawdle a bit, because if they'd hurried straight back to the flat, it could have been disastrous.

The first thing they noticed was the kitchen floor, which was covered with Fru-Grains.

"What the . . ." began Joey. Then he saw Sir Quentin on the coffee table, a paw to his lips. Hush.

For the first time since they'd known him, Sir Quentin spoke in a rapid burst of MSL, ending with signs simple enough for the humans to understand. Pointing to a watercolor painting labeled *St. Paul's Cathedral at Dawn*. Pointing at an ear. Paw to lips. Hush. *St. Paul's Cathedral at Dawn* is listening.

Now Sir Quentin was making the unmistakable signs for "Follow me!" and he headed for the bathroom. With one last sign. Bring the Thumbtop that Jake had left on the coffee table. Megan and Joey followed him into the bathroom, but not before Megan had said clearly in the direction of *St. Paul's Cathedral at Dawn*, "I'm going to take a shower."

Inside the bathroom they closed the door, and Megan started the shower running, the way she'd seen it done in movies to cover up whispered conversations. Then she sat with Joey on the edge of the bathtub while Sir Quentin stood on the counter to tell them what had happened.

"I was at the window," he said, "contemplating the Mother of Parliaments and trying to remember the fourth and fifth lines of the poem that William Wordsworth penned when observing this view. It had just come to me:

> *The city now doth like a garment wear*
> *The beauty of the morning: silent, bare*

Suddenly, he said, his view of the Houses of Parliament was blocked by a hand—a human hand on the windowpane. Sir Quentin ran to hide under the couch and watched as a whole human appeared on the balcony. Watched as that human prized open the window. Watched as he took down St. Paul's Cathedral at Dawn, and started doing something to the back of it.

"As you may well imagine," he said, "my poor heart was all aflutter."

"And then?" prompted Megan.

And then? Deep down, of course, Sir Quentin was a mouse, and the modern mouse is hardwired at times of danger to apply the full force of his, or her, intelligence to any threatening situation.

And what popped into Sir Quentin's brain was the need to get a record of what was happening. Or as he put it, "I was felicitously placed to record the phenomena that I beheld, even though such an activity might result in danger to my person."

Jake's Thumbtop was still on the coffee table, so while the man was busy with the picture, Sir Quentin crept out from under the couch, activated the Thumbtop's camera function, and pushed the button to take three or four pictures before sprinting back under the couch to hide.

Joey clicked his way to the recent photos on the Thumbtop.

They were tiny, of course, but when Megan pulled out her magnifying glass she could see the round head of a man who was bald on top, his face framed in a beard.

And a ripple of fear started at her toes, ran up her body, and exploded in her brain—almost like the fear she'd felt last summer when someone seemed to be stalking her clear across the continent. Who was that bald guy? Who knew they were in this apartment? Did Faceless now have a face?

"Do you think he bugged anything else?" she asked. "Anything except that picture?"

"That might indeed have been his intention, were I not present," said Sir Quentin. "He had several pens in his pocket, which struck me as suspicious."

"Could be spy pens," said Joey. "A kid in my English class has one. Did he spread them around?"

"He was denied that opportunity," said Sir Quentin, "for I was not about to permit further infelicitous intrusions."

"So you bit him?" asked Megan.

Sir Quentin shuddered. "Biting is not in my nature," he

said. "Indeed, I trust that I will go to my grave without having inflicted upon myself the taste of human flesh. No, I chose instead to play upon fears to which I believe the British are prone—fears of 'ghoulies and ghosties and long-leggity beasties and things that go bump in the night.'"

"Huh?" said Joey.

Sir Quentin was enjoying himself. "It is I believe a saying that originated in Cornwall." He pointed upriver. "The narrow peninsula at the southwestern corner of this blessed isle, where beasties abound. To implement my scheme, I made my way to the kitchen, where a container was fortuitously placed adjacent to the edge of the counter. I crept toward it." He demonstrated by crouching down and ooching along for a few steps. "Then I pushed it off the counter. Nearby was a glass jar that I caused to slide until it gathered sufficient momentum to fly into a rack of utensils, with resulting reverberations."

"And?" Megan prompted.

"Peering into the living room," continued Sir Quentin, "I espied the human casting a look of profound anxiety in the direction of those sounds as if he indeed suspected the presence of beasties. Then he removed himself from the premises. In other words, he skedaddled."

Julia, who normally found Sir Quentin tiresome in the extreme, rushed over to him and looked as if she was about to give him the hip-to-hip bump that mice use to congratulate each other—until at the last moment she held out a paw for him to shake instead.

"That was so cool, dude," said Joey.

"We'd better get rid of whatever's behind that picture," said Megan. "Before Mom and Jake get back."

Trey cleared his throat, which usually meant he had a better idea than any human but didn't want to seem too pushy.

"Presumably, it's a voice-activated microphone," he said. "And your parents may want to leave it there, so they can give it wrong information. Like a red herring."

Which made sense, as Trey's suggestions usually did.

"I'll wait for them downstairs," said Joey. "I'll tell them what's happened."

"Let's both go," said Megan. There was no way she was going to be left alone in this apartment. Not now.

As they came out of the bathroom Megan sang out, "Now for that nap."

"Me too," said Joey. "Man, I'm *so* tired."

Then he opened the front door as silently as he could, and they both slipped out. When Susie and Jake walked back from Sir Brian's apartment ten minutes later they found Megan and Joey on a bench, with a Thumbtop between them in case the mice who were on watch in their apartment sounded the alarm.

chapter ten

The four Humans Who Knew had to act normal, of course—in body language at least—in case someone was watching.

For Megan and Joey, this meant that while their words told their parents of burglars and bugs and spies and the bravery of mice, their bodies had to pretend they'd been waiting to drag the adults off to the riverside walk, pointing excitedly at the London Eye, the massive Ferris wheel that dominates that part of the city.

And the parents had to confine themselves to hugs for Megan and Joey that were no bigger than normal, even though they were both shattered by the thought that the kids could have been in the apartment when a stranger came through the window.

"Loggocorp!" wailed Susie. "How did they know we were here?"

"Followed us, I guess," said Jake, giving her shoulders a squeeze. "Followed you. So now we have to shake them off. Find somewhere safe."

"But where can we go?" asked Megan, remembering to grin for whoever might be watching. "What's safe anymore?"

"Mice will find a place," said Jake. "Right, Ken?"

"You got it, mate," came a muffled voice from his pocket. "But first you'd better think of what you're gonna say to that there recording device, yeah?"

As they walked back along the river, trying to look casual, they concocted a dialogue for the benefit of St. Paul's Cathedral at Dawn. It went like this:

Susie [entering apartment]: Hi, guys! Good to be home!
(*sound of bedroom door opening.*)
Joey: Hi, Mom! Hi, Dad! (*loud yawn*). Been taking a nap.
Megan (*yawning*): Me too.
Joey: I'm hungry. There's nothing to eat here except that
    cereal. And look—Megan knocked it over.
Megan: I did *not*. It was Joey. Must have been. Why does
    he always—
Susie: Hey, you guys, cool it.
Jake: Let me tell you about your mom, Megan. Sir Brian

was so impressed with her paper on hairy-nosed wombats. She asked him for suggestions, but he thought it was perfect. Just about ready to publish.

Susie: So now that little job's out of the way, we can forget about wombats and Sir Brian and have a great time. Why don't I book a ride on the London Eye for tomorrow? Then on Friday we can go to the Palace, see what the Queen's got to show us.

Joey: And a soccer game, Dad? Can we go to a soccer game? Chelsea's playing Manchester United on Wednesday.

It was a strain, giving *St. Paul's Cathedral at Dawn* the impression they'd stay in this apartment for at least a week, when in reality there was only one thing to do. Don't even unpack. Get out of here. Now.

There had to be one last scene for the benefit of *St. Paul's Cathedral at Dawn*: the scene that prepared it to expect silence for at least a few hours. So just before the humans picked up all their belongings and left, they told each other (and the picture) that they were heading out to eat, after which they would find a tour bus to take them on a long, slow ride around London.

And in case *St. Paul's Cathedral at Dawn* could measure the wavelengths of voices and tell that some were not human, no mouse uttered a peep until they were in the car.

Just to be on the safe side, Jake drove south for a couple of blocks first and ducked into side streets as mice surveyed the traffic from the back window, making sure they were not being followed. Then he drove north across Vauxhall Bridge and pulled into a parking space so they could catch their breath and find out what part of England they should head for next.

It was Ken who spoke first, from the cupholder he was sharing with Sir Quentin.

"Who'd have thought it?" he said. "Getting rumbled like that. And you know what? If it hadn't been for this guy"—he gave Sir Quentin a thump on the back—"we'd have been dead meat! I was thinkin' you was a bit of a stuffed shirt, know what I mean? Didn't expect no heroics."

"Heroics?" said Sir Quentin. "I accept your adulation in the spirit in which it was undoubtedly meant. However, notwithstanding appearances—perhaps I should say notwithstanding the evidence of my speech—I am at heart a mouse, and will therefore always endeavor to act for the preservation of my Nation and of the bi-species enterprise in which we are engaged."

"Yeah, yeah, yeah," said Ken. "I get it. Once a mouse, always a mouse. And you didn't want to let those guys get away with it. Still, that was good stuff, me old codger."

And Sir Quentin did not seem to take offense.

Susie reached out to pat him on the back.

"I know how much you wanted to see London," she said. "Let's hope we have some time after this meeting to go to the Tower and Buckingham Palace. Things like that."

"You deserve it, Sir Q," said Jake. "You are one brave mouse. Who knows what those guys would have found out if you hadn't been there. Let's see the picture you took. See if it gives us any clues."

He fished out his Thumbtop, clicked to the photo, and showed it around, as one magnifying glass after another peered at it.

It still looked like any old burglar. The bald man in jeans and sneakers and a hoodie, his face framed by a beard.

For a moment Megan wished her mom was, well, just a mom. Someone who didn't stick her neck out. Not a famous climate scientist who got herself followed.

"Don't worry, Megan," said Jake soothingly. "No way they're following us now. And we'll find somewhere *really* safe to stay until the meeting starts. Right, Ken?"

"You got it," said Ken, who'd been working on Susie's

Thumbtop. "My Headquarters says you can go straight to that secret meeting place now, yeah? A bit early, like. Somewhere safe as houses, as we says over here. They've given me a link and . . ."

He clicked and his mouth fell open, then he staggered backward, as if blinded by what he saw.

"Cor blimey," he said. "Stone the crows! Did I say 'safe as houses'? Safe as palaces, more like."

At the word *palaces* Sir Quentin ran forward to peer at the screen.

"Oh, my stars!" he said. "Do my poor eyes deceive me? Or is that indeed Buckford Hall? Home of the Duke of Wiltshire, sixteenth of that ilk?"

Jake reached down for the Thumbtop.

"Holy Toledo," he said. "Kids, you are not going to believe this."

It was indeed a palace, a massive house with at least forty windows facing them, flanked by two round towers.

"One of our best stately homes," said Ken proudly. "Yer can't get much statelier, to be honest. The old duke what owns it lives in one of them towers now, and most of the rest is for conferences and such, for the bread and honey. By which I mean money, to keep the place up. And what makes it so great? I'll tell you what makes it so great. The old duke wants his guests to think they're still in the nineteenth century! That's his gimmick, like. There's no Internet, and your phones won't work there neither, so no hacking problem for you."

"Won't that make it hard to do business at all?" asked Susie. "I mean, what if we need to get in touch with Coconut Man's relative? Or Cleveland?"

"I was coming to that," said Ken, as he read to the end of the e-mail from his Headquarters. "There's something else that there duke don't allow."

He gazed around the car, as if waiting for guesses.

"Cats!" he said triumphantly. "His Grace is allergic! So we got one thousand three hundred and eighty-one guys there at the last count, yeah? Biggest clan in the country, I reckon. And they've got Thumbtops with satellite connections, so no worries. You'll be able to communicate all you want. Oh, and one other thing," Ken added, looking around to make sure he had everyone's full attention. "To be extra secret, like, your meeting isn't about rain forests at all."

"Huh?" said Jake and Susie together.

"What's big and wet and getting a bit closer all the time, from that there climate change?" asked Ken.

"The ocean?" Megan guessed.

"Got it in one, my love," said Ken, doing a somewhat cramped pirouette in his cupholder. "That's what my Headquarters has booked you in as. Sir Brian Mason's Sea-Level Task Force."

As Ken gave Jake directions to Buckford Hall, Megan sank back in her corner, so glad that mice were in control again. She tried to imagine their arrival at the massive palace, wondering if it would be anything like the television series she'd sometimes watched with her mom, where maids and footmen lined up at the entrance bowing to visitors. One footman. Two footmen. Three footmen. . . .

Before the car had even reached the suburbs of London she was deep into a sleep that should have happened at thirty-five thousand feet, ten hours ago. And while she was asleep Trey used her Thumbtop to write to Headquarters and tell the Big Cheese everything that had happened.

It was still early in Cleveland, and as he did most mornings, weather permitting, the Big Cheese was taking a stroll on his balcony.

It was one of the best things about the new Headquarters, that balcony. It had been Mr. Fred's idea—to drill a mouse-sized hole through the wall of the Big Cheese's office, with a flap on it to keep out the drafts. Now for the first time in his life the leader of the Mouse Nation could go outside whenever he had the urge. Sniff the breeze. Feel the warmth of the sun.

This morning, as always, the Big Cheese sent a couple of muscle mice through the hole first to check for hawks. When they signaled that the coast was clear, he followed them outside, breathing deep in the crisp air, admiring the last bright leaves of fall against a deep blue sky.

One of his morning pleasures was to look down on The Fishery and speculate about what might be going on there. A couple of weeks ago, Mr. Jake had happened to glance up and must have seen that a mouse was peering down at him, because he waved. Now the Big Cheese looked forward to that wave every day.

This was such a great change, since the days at the old Headquarters in Silicon Valley! There, he seldom, if ever, saw a human. The larger species was an abstraction, known mainly through the Internet. Sometimes the Big Cheese had even privately wished that he could have been an ordinary mouse, a run-of-the-mill mouse in daily contact with a host family, so he could observe that species at close range. But living next to the Fishers was almost as good—which was why he felt a little empty this morning, as empty as the silent house he gazed down on.

He was still looking at it when a secretary mouse came

barreling through the hole and onto the balcony. An e-mail had just arrived from Trey, Talking Mouse Three.

"Why would he e-mail me?" asked the Big Cheese. "He knows he can make an appointment to speak to me any time."

A shiver went through the secretary mouse. His boss didn't *know*? The news of the Great Smuggling Adventure had zipped through Headquarters at the speed of light, but no one had dared tell the *boss*?

The secretary mouse quickly ran back through the hole in case he caught any blame once the Big Cheese learned the truth. Because there'd be more than enough blame to go around, right? Blame that could fall not only on the three absent mice, who'd left their posts without permission, but also on all those at Headquarters who had known the truth but hadn't told their leader.

The Big Cheese followed the secretary mouse into his office and found the Director of Security waiting for him. And although the director was trying to look stern, his paws kept coming up to his face in the fleeting sign for "Smile" (a paw to each corner of the mouth, pulling outward).

"Something's amusing you?" asked the Big Cheese.

Puzzled, he read Trey's e-mail about spies in London, and the efficiency of the British branch of the Mouse Nation, and a drive deep into the countryside. Now the truth filtered through the words. That at least Trey, and possibly others, had smuggled themselves to Britain without permission.

Of course he had to pretend to be outraged, so he thundered, "They will be punished for this," because that was expected of him. But he turned away so the director couldn't see his own paws stretching the corners of his mouth outward in a smile. Partly it was a smile of relief. Although the Big Cheese trusted his humans most of the time, he'd had some doubts about sending them off on such a delicate mission without adequate mouse support. Given Loggocorp's reputation for ruthlessness, it was good to know that Trey was in charge. Of all talking mice, he was the one most likely to keep his head in an emergency. And as it was now clear from his e-mail, emergencies were all too likely to happen.

cHapter eLeveN

here were no rows of bowing servants to welcome the humans to Buckford Hall. Just one man in a footman's livery who opened the massive front door and gazed with horror at the four Americans, whose clothes looked as if they had been slept in (which they had).

"I'm afraid you have made a mistake," he said. "Tours of the house are over for the season."

He started to close the massive door, but Jake stuck a foot in it.

"We're expected," he said. "We're here for the sea-level meeting. Where do we check in?"

"I regret to inform you, sir," said the footman, "that registration for that meeting does not take place for two days. I am told that the public house in the village provides a reasonable bed-and-breakfast."

Megan put her hand in her pocket and gave Trey a little squeeze. Was it possible that the British mice hadn't managed to fix the reservation after all? That they simply weren't good at that sort of thing?

"Now, wait just one minute," said Jake. "I think if you check your bookings—"

The footman gave a courtly bow that Megan recognized. It was the one Sir Quentin used when he wanted to imply that even if you thought you had won an argument, you really hadn't.

The footman left the door open while he whispered to someone who looked like a butler, who whispered to another footman, who vanished behind the huge staircase that soared upward from the entrance hall, wide enough to drive a horse and carriage up and down.

It didn't take long for a man in a business suit to bustle out from behind the stairs and almost run toward them.

"Oh, Mr. and Mrs. Fisher, welcome! Welcome!" He glared at the footman. "Please accept my apologies for the misunderstanding. My name is Peabody, and I have just been informed of your early arrival. Your reservation is for the deluxe package, which means you will be housed in the Royal Suite. It is where King George the Fourth once stayed on his travels around the kingdom and where Queen Victoria herself was once accommodated, so I trust that it will meet with your approval."

The four humans looked at each other. Deluxe package? Royal Suite? How had mice pulled that one off?

Mr. Peabody turned to one of the footmen.

"When you have unloaded the luggage, take the car down to the parking lot. You may have seen the sign, sir," he said to Jake. "No vehicles may remain on the grounds."

"What, even for houseguests?" asked Jake.

"For everyone," said Mr. Peabody. "His Grace chooses to provide his guests with an experience free of distracting devices such as the automobile and the telephone. Now, if you will follow me."

He led the way through a series of rooms that looked more like museum setups than places where humans could actually live. Red ropes kept visitors marching in a straight line under ceilings where cupids frolicked, past huge pictures where figures from ancient myths did strange things.

At last they reached a massive door leading to a spiral staircase.

"I apologize for the fact that we have no lift in the South Tower," said Mr. Peabody. "His Grace has installed one in the North Tower for his own use because he is unfortunately not as mobile as he once was."

With footmen carrying their bags, the four humans climbed up the spiral stairs to the Royal Suite. Here a massive bedroom occupied half the space of the tower, and a magnificent sitting room the other half. Mr. Peabody waited until everyone had finished exclaiming over the view from the windows in the rounded wall. The magnificence of the four-poster bed. The beauty of the tapestries that lined the walls. The bathtub as big as a Volkswagen Beetle (in a bathroom the size of a garage). Then he led them all up one floor to see two smaller bedrooms. Smaller, yes, but still vast by Cleveland standards, and lined with dark tapestries in which archers shot at animals that seemed to be leaping out of the walls to escape.

"I will leave you now," said Mr. Peabody. "A footman will be here at seven twenty to escort you to dinner. It will be served promptly at seven thirty, and His Grace will be present."

"His Grace?" said Susie. (Actually more "squeaked" than "said.")

Mr. Peabody inclined his head.

"The deluxe package," he said, "includes one dinner with the duke."

"But we didn't bring a lot of clothes," said Jake. "Are we meant to get all dressed up for dinner?"

Mr. Peabody looked a little pained.

"Dinner jackets are not required," he said. "His Grace

understands that Americans favor less formal attire. However," he added, looking sideways at Joey's Cleveland Browns T-shirt, "for the gentlemen, a tie is de rigueur."

Meaning tux, no—tie, yes.

As soon as Mr. Peabody had given a final courtly bow and left, the humans gathered in the big sitting room. Almost immediately there was movement behind one of the tapestries and two mice emerged, followed by a nervous-looking gaggle of twenty smaller ones who could only be a Youth Chorus.

One of the adult mice—one with a blue thread around his neck marking him as a director—launched into a dance of MSL that seemed to Megan to be a bit more restrained in its swoops and waggles than the speech of American mice.

Ken ran forward to translate, but at his first words, "This here's the Director of Hospitality and he's saying . . ." Sir Quentin rushed to stand in front of him.

"Allow me to translate," he said. "The Director of Hospitality, for this is indeed he, would bid you bend an ear, or an eye, to the dulcet moves of the Youth Chorus under the direction of the Master of Mouse Musick. That's musick with a 'k,'" he added sternly, glaring at his humans as if they might contradict, "maintaining the orthography preferred for centuries by the nobility of this great realm."

The Master of Mouse Musick waved his baton and the

Youth Chorus lurched and waggled and swayed into song as Sir Quentin translated:

> Hip hip hurrah
> For friends afar
> From lands beyond
> Our little pond
> Each honored guest
> To us is best.

Megan had heard a number of mouse "songs for all occasions" since her welcome to the Headquarters of the Mouse Nation almost a year ago, and she knew they were seldom meant to be funny, but all the humans had a hard time keeping straight faces at the lines:

> Now let us pray
> You'll save the day
> If humans bungle
> Protecting jungle.

"Thank you, thank you," said Jake, his voice a bit strained from trying not to laugh. "We are indeed honored. Now if the Director of Hospitality can answer a few questions?"

"Indeed," said the director.

"First, how did your clan swing the deluxe package thing?" asked Jake.

"Fortunately the computer for conference bookings—the only computer His Grace allows on the premises—was unguarded during the lunch hour," said the mouse. "We were thus able to enhance your application for early arrival."

"Of course," said Susie with a laugh, "Mr. and Mrs. Fisher, Nobel Prize winners."

"The Nobel was not mentioned," said the director, who like American mice had a hard time telling when humans were kidding. "However, the fact that your conference involves climate change was of interest to His Grace, as we knew it would be. He has some concern about the future of the planet, of which he owns a sizable share."

"That's great!" said Susie. "Though I'm not sure he'll want to eat with us when he finds out we don't have anything like the right clothes! Joey, did you bring a single shirt with buttons?"

Sir Quentin spun around to face her.

"Let not sartorial deficiencies sabotage this social opportunity," he said, "one that may have been previously enjoyed by no human from the city of Cleveland—nay, from the whole state of Ohio. With your customary skill at adaptation, I feel sure that adequate garments may be contrived."

"What about us?" asked Ken. "Anyone think about food for us? Bit of nosh, eh?"

"Have no fear," said the director. "You and your colleagues are invited to dine with us below stairs, at the invitation of the Brigadier, leader of our clan."

"Below stairs!" wailed Sir Quentin. "We are to dine adjacent to the servants' quarters?"

"Aw," said Joey, who often found Sir Quentin a pain, "and you were expecting to maybe eat with the duke?"

"You may mock, sirrah," said Sir Quentin crisply, "but I must confess that the opportunity to view a person of his rank at close quarters would indeed be a high point in my poor life."

"Oh, let Sir Quentin come with us," said Susie. "He can hide in my bag. It's already got a good viewing hole, for when Savannah comes to work with me. Is that okay with everyone?"

There were no objections—and indeed Megan had a hunch that Trey and Julia might be glad of an evening free of Sir Quentin.

"We shall take our leave," said the director, as Trey translated. "And remember, if you want anything, anything at all, just pull the bell and a human will appear. It's like magic!" he added. "Happens every time."

The director vanished behind the tapestry, leaving the

humans gazing at the bellpull hanging near the fireplace. Tug on it and a human appears?

It was Joey who gave in first. He just couldn't resist. And indeed a maid appeared bringing a tray of tea and cake, followed by a footman who lit the fire in the grate, followed by another maid asking if the ladies required any help in dressing for dinner with the duke. And right behind her was a valet offering to lay out the clothing that the gentlemen would wear for the occasion. Even if there really wasn't much. Jake's only jacket was the leather one he lived in most of the time, and all the valet could lay out for Joey was a clean T-shirt and a tie borrowed from his dad.

chapter twelve

After the humans and Sir Quentin set off for their dinner with the duke, a guide led Trey, Julia and Ken down through the walls to Mouse Hall, the headquarters of the Buckford clan—all thirteen hundred and eighty-one members of it.

"Stone the crows!" Ken whispered, as the three were led into the hall. "Knock me down with a feather."

Mouse Hall was located in the crawl space near the kitchen. It was an imposing room, lit now by a string of white Christmas tree lights that the mice had patched into the main electricity supply.

The walls were lined with pieces of rich, dark fabric.

"I see you are admiring our tapestries," said the Brigadier as he stepped forward to greet his guests. "We were fortunate in that the late duchess was fond of turning unwanted fabric into bed coverings—into quilts. Mice from my Department of Interior Decorating were always on the lookout for pieces that would serve our purposes."

In the center of the room was a table made from a piece of stiff cardboard, propped up on old spools that had once held thread and covered now with a white human handkerchief. It was laid for dinner, with bottle caps for plates. The Brigadier sat at the head of the table, while Julia was shown to the place at his right, and Trey and Ken sat to his left. Although the food was good (with a cheese called Cornish Yarg that was the best Julia and Trey had ever tasted) the conversation was stilted. Small talk, of the type that American mice usually don't bother with. The Brigadier chatted about the weather, and the best types of local cheese, and the goings-on of the British royal family, and the Brigadier's hobby of collecting bottle caps.

"We'd love to see your collection," Trey lied, and as he'd hoped, a guide mouse was summoned to rescue them from the dining room. He led them to a side chamber where several hundred bottle caps gleamed in the half light, and from there the three could escape to the IT room. Here, a half-dozen Thumbtops were linked to an antenna that snaked up through a ventilation grille to communicate with a satellite.

"Can we e-mail?" asked Julia, who felt the special pain of

mice separated from their clan and longed to be in touch with Larry and Curly.

"Better than that," said Ken. "Look!"

The IT mice had already made a video connection on one of the Thumbtops, and three familiar mice had appeared on its screen—Savannah, plus one mouse with one dot on his ear, and another with three. Curly and Larry.

"Greetings, Mouselings," said Savannah, pushing her nose at the webcam so it looked huge. "How's my Treyzy Weyzy?"

She gave the webcam a big, wet kiss. Trey took a step back and looked around, as if she must surely be talking to someone else, but saw that the damage had been done. Every English mouse in the room was making the "Laughing out loud" sign.

"Enough of that," Trey said as crisply as he could. "We have urgent business to conduct. First, Julia would like a brief chat with Curly and Larry. And while that is going on, Savannah, could you please take a message to our leader? Tell him we need to know if he has any special orders for us."

There was just time for Julia to tell her clan brothers that she was fine, and for them to tell her that Larry's sports report had been changed into a comedy routine—which was odd because Larry had never shown much sense of humor. Then Curly and Larry were nudged out of the way by the Big Cheese's personal guard of muscle mice, and he took their place.

"Greetings, mouse!" he said to Trey. "When you return, we will discuss your behavior. I was most displeased to learn that you had left your post here without permission. For now, however, you may give your humans some good news. I can confirm that they will meet at least one member of Coconut Man's family soon after the experts arrive at Buckford Hall the day after tomorrow. Meanwhile the humans can relax, and enjoy that extraordinary place."

Relax? Enjoy? Well, yes and no.

It was a workout for the four humans, following a footman to dinner, with Sir Quentin tucked into Susie's handbag. Down the stairs of the South Tower they went, then through an even longer parade of rooms than before, all with the red velvet ropes to keep visitors from mauling the artifacts—a pink breakfast room, a green morning room, a gold salon, a blue drawing room. Finally they reached the main dining room, where a table big enough for fifty guests gleamed under the eyes of past dukes, looking hungrily out from their paintings.

At the far end of the table, five places were set, with two footmen stationed where they could help the honored guests to sit and eat. And as the four Americans reached their places, a man with white hair and a bristly white mustache came barreling into the dining hall in an electric wheelchair, much too fast. He jammed on the brakes and skidded to such an abrupt stop that his glasses flew onto the table.

"Dratted contraption!" he roared. "My advice to you, don't get old. Soon as I hit seventy-eight my legs stopped working."

Sir Quentin peered eagerly through the hole in Susie's handbag for his first sighting of a real British aristocrat, the subspecies of human that he considered superior to all others.

More than any other American mouse—quite possibly, more than any mouse in the world—Sir Quentin knew his dukes. He knew they were almost at the top of the pecking order of British nobility, below kings and queens but above earls and way, way, way above barons. And though he knew, deep down, that this duke would be wearing none of the outward signs of nobility—no ermine robe, no coronet—he hadn't expected this. Not a wheelchair out of control. Not the pink face. Not glasses flying off. Not a suit that was a little shiny from wear in some places.

The duke had turned his protruding blue eyes on his guests, and they seemed to protrude a bit more when they reached Joey, whose overlong tie hung from his bare neck over his Oregon Ducks T-shirt. Surely, thought Sir Quentin, this must be the time for the duke to show his stuff. To exercise some authority.

And indeed the duke made a sound like "harrumph," half astonishment, half laughter—perhaps the cue for the footmen to *do* something. Maybe remove the young human from the gracious presence? Banish him from this magnificent room and provide him with sustenance in the servants' quarters?

But what the duke said was, "Jolly good show, what? Trust you Yanks to be 'with it.' Isn't that what the young sprogs say these days? Bit hard to keep up with the lingo."

And what the duke *did* was—in Sir Quentin's view—even less appropriate.

"Ralph!" he called out to the nearest footman. "Be a good chap and fetch me a shirt from the gift shop. One like his," he added, pointing at Joey.

One footman left the dining room and the other leapt forward to remove the duke's jacket and unbutton his shirt.

And Sir Quentin turned away from his hole, because you could now see much more duke than any mouse would care to, a pudgy expanse of duke, until the footman came rushing in with a T-shirt reading, "I ♥ Buckford Hall," and pulled it down over His Grace's head.

"Much better, what?" said the duke, after he'd fought his way into the T-shirt and the footman adjusted his tie on top of it. "Ridiculous rules we have. Made to be broken, don't you know. Can't have you Yanks thinking I'm an anachronism, living in a place like this." He turned to Megan. "You know what anachronism means, young lady?"

Megan silently thanked Sir Quentin because it was indeed a word he used quite frequently. "Out of date," she said.

He laughed. "Good show. Ridiculous, isn't it? Didn't do anything to earn all this." He waved his hand around the magnificent room and the ceiling where cupids flew through the air, their bare bottoms gleaming in an unearthly light. "Just a matter of luck, getting born here. But I'll take it," he said, leaning forward and lowering his voice, "because I get to choose my own grub. Whatever I want to eat."

And the grub—the food—turned out to be the duke's old favorites from his days at boarding school. Brown soup that tasted mostly of salt. Roast beef cooked until it was dry and dark brown through and through. Mushy Brussels sprouts and lumpy mashed potatoes.

As a footman leaned over to offer him the Brussels sprouts, Jake approached a question that had been hovering in Megan's head too.

"When people come to conferences, er, do you . . ."

"Feed them this stuff? Good heavens, no." The duke put a Brussels sprout on the table and flicked it at Joey. "Don't want to waste it on them! Peabody hired a French chef for the conference business."

"Do you have conferences all year round?" asked Jake.

"If I can," said the duke. "Two or three at a time. Helps me keep the old place up, what? I need the lolly. Conferences, and the day-trippers tramping through the house in summer. Lucky I have my tower. One place I can hide."

"Two or three conferences?" asked Susie. "So will there be others here at the same time as ours?"

"Only some quilters," said the duke, scraping some gravy off the heart on his shirt. "Coming in tomorrow. My late wife was fascinated by quilts, so we often have groups of them, quilting away. Harmless, what?"

Megan saw Jake and her mom look at each other and smile. Yes, quilters sounded harmless. You never heard of quilters spying.

"Your group's the most interesting I've had for a while," said the duke. "Your Sir Brian, I saw him on the telly, talking about the forests in Brazil. Saving the seas now, is he? Good for him. I don't like what's happening to the climate, don't like it at all. Storms like we never used to have. New pests in my wheat fields. Cuckoos coming earlier and earlier."

"Well, let's hope Sir Brian can fix it, Your Lordship," said Jake.

"Your Grace," said Susie.

Then the duke said something that almost made Sir Quentin faint. "Let's forget that 'Your Grace' nonsense. My name's William, and you can call me Billy."

Sir Quentin sank down to the bottom of the handbag while his worldview on dukes rearranged itself. T-shirts? Brussels sprouts? *Billy?* When he peered through the hole again, the topic of conversation had changed and His Grace—Billy!—was talking to Miss Megan and Mr. Joey.

"What are you youngsters going to do while your parents are saving the planet?" he asked. "Do you ride?"

"Ride what?" asked Joey. "Skateboards?"

The duke leaned back in his chair to laugh, looking up at the footmen to share the joke. "Zebras!" he roared. "Elephants!

No, horses, of course. That's what we ride around here."

"Megan knows how to ride," said her mom. "She had her own steed for a couple of years. Good old Charlie."

Charlie. Yes, you had to say "steed" because Charlie wasn't exactly a horse but the old mule who'd worked for them on the Atlantic island, bringing supplies up to their hillside cabin from the little port.

And, yes, Megan had often ridden on Charlie as he wandered around looking for new patches of grass to munch. If you could call it riding, when you were sitting on an animal who didn't take commands from anyone on top but only from humans in front (a pull on the halter) or behind (a sharp slap on the rump).

"Well, good for you," said the duke, and turned to a footman. "John, set it up with the groom, there's a good chap. Tell him to find a suitable mount for this young lady tomorrow. And a nice quiet pony for her brother."

Looking at Joey's anxious face, Megan thought that for once this might be something she could do slightly better than he could, because as far as she knew he'd never been on any sort of horse in his life. And at least Charlie had been the right shape.

chapter thirteen

hen dessert came (something called spot-ted dog, a doughy lump decorated with raisins) the duke was asking Susie about her own work.

She got so excited describing her research on wild sheep and endangered wombats that she knocked her handbag off the back of her chair. A footman picked it up and hung it from the chair-back again. But now it was the wrong way round, and Sir Quentin could no longer see through his spy-hole.

This happened just as the topic changed from endangered wombats to the endangered nobility of England.

"Not sure how long we'll be around, don't you know," the duke said. "You hear a lot of grumbling these days. People think it doesn't make sense to get a title just because your daddy had one. And I must say, some of my ancestors didn't exactly deserve it. Like that chap."

He pointed at the portrait of a man in a curly white wig, surrounded by hunting dogs.

"He was a rogue, if ever there was one. Some sort of scandal at court. And that chap."

He pointed to a duke in a naval uniform who was clutching a three-colored spaniel as if it were a stuffed toy, his gaze seemingly fixed on distant horizons.

"A bit soft in the head, that one," said the duke. "He was the twelfth duke, but—EEEEK!"

Determined to see the ancestors in question, Sir Quentin had stuck his head out of the top of Susie's bag, only to find himself gazing straight into the pale blue eyes of the duke. Then Sir Quentin felt himself being wrapped in fingers. Gloved fingers. Footman fingers.

"Little devil," said the duke. "Gave me quite a turn. Must have climbed into your bag when you weren't looking!"

"Don't worry, Your Grace, I'll put it down the toilet," said the footman, but Megan was quick, oh so quick, to jump up and grab the footman's arm and say that the mouse was her pet, she was sorry, *so* sorry, for smuggling him in.

"Pet mouse, eh?" said the duke. Megan held Sir Quentin out so they could gaze at each other, mouse and duke, and Megan could feel the mouse heart beating faster than usual, racing with the excitement of what? A near-death experience? Or being formally introduced to a duke, even if it was a duke in an "I ♥ Buckford Hall" T-shirt?

"Dear little chap," said the duke. "I don't mind them myself. Must have hundreds of mice in this place. Cook wanted a cat, but I wouldn't allow it. Cats make me sneeze." He lowered his voice and peered at the four Americans. "The other day, Peabody found a mouse in his shoe! I thought he might resign!"

Megan was still cradling Sir Quentin, ready to hold his jaws shut if he forgot the routine for What Would a Pet Mouse Do, and maybe came out with something he'd learned at the Talking Academy, like smiling, or a burst of Shakespeare.

But she needn't have worried. Sir Quentin was wriggling around in her hand, doing a convincing imitation of a mouse who was trying to get away.

"Expect he'd like some of our spotted dog, would he?" asked the duke.

"We could try," said Megan, and put Sir Quentin down on the table with a piece of her spotted dog in front of him, corralling him with her arms. A chance, finally, for Sir Quentin to dine with a duke, even if it was only on spotted dog, and even if he couldn't say a word, pretending to be trapped in Megan's encircling arms, pretending to like the food in front of him.

. . . .

Two minutes after the humans made it back to the sitting room in the South Tower, there was a slight swaying of tapestries before three mice came hurtling out to greet them.

"You. Would. Not. Believe. What it's like down there," said Trey, as Megan bent down to pick him up.

"Yeah, bit of all right, wasn't it?" said Ken who had hung back, with no human of his own to welcome him. "Lovely nosh, that was."

"Not just the food," said Trey. And he described the table with its sparkling white cloth. The tapestries. And best of all, the satellite connection.

"And we got a bit of a surprise from that, yeah?" said Ken. "Something for our pal Treyzy Weyzy."

Mice don't blush, of course, but they sometimes seem to shrink when they're embarrassed, and now Trey went down by a mouse size or two. It didn't help that Ken was dancing around in circles on the coffee table, making kissing noises.

"Don't tell me," said Susie. "Savannah."

"Savannah," mumbled Trey, hiding his face in Megan's neck.

"C'mon," said Joey, reaching out to Megan's shoulder to tickle Trey behind the ears. "You're among friends now, Treyzy Weyzy."

"Very funny, very funny," said Trey, as icily as he knew how. "But after we'd talked to Savannah we actually had a serious conversation with the Big Cheese. Anyone interested in serious conversations? Anyone at all?"

"Of course, Trey," said Jake. Then he spoiled it by picking up a tapestry cushion and pressing it to his face while his shoulders shook.

Trey waited a moment until his humans came back to earth.

"It was about security," he said. "You remember? That nice thing we didn't have, in London?"

And yes, that fixed the giggles. Fast. It pulled the humans back from the world of tapestries and footmen and spotted dogs as Trey passed on his leader's message. That all was well. They could relax. And a descendant of Coconut Man was definitely due to appear in two or three days' time.

At last the clock agreed that it was a respectable time for the humans to put their jet lag to bed. Susie came upstairs with Megan to tuck her in. Megan wished her mom could stick around until she fell asleep, as she used to do on the island. Somebody had lit a fire, and its light flickered spookily over the looming figures in the tapestries—here an archer with his bow drawn back, there a snarling wild boar, looking by this dim light as if it might charge oinking out of the tapestry to get her.

This was foolish. It had been at least three years since

Megan last felt afraid of the dark, and she so much didn't want to go whimpering to her mom, particularly if it meant navigating that dimly lit spiral staircase.

"Don't worry," said Trey. "We'll keep watch, me and Julia."

It was good that he could read her mind sometimes, and the feeling of his warmth against her neck was comforting, but mice against wild boars? Mice against the ghoulies and ghosties and long-leggity beasties that Sir Quentin said roamed this island? She decided to close her eyes and count to twenty and if she still felt scared after that . . .

She never got to twenty. By the time she reached twelve, jet lag took over, and she slept. And Trey and Julia, exhausted, slept too.

The night would probably have been beastie-free had it not been for Megan's fame among mice. There was no way that the members of the Buckford Hall clan would pass up a chance like this—having the most famous human in the world (among mice) in their midst. Yes, with their human here for three or four days most of them could expect to catch a glimpse of her, but why wait? Left to themselves, almost all the 1,310 mice in the clan would have rushed up through the walls right then, to see Megan sleeping. But as their leaders knew, any mass swarming of mice can be sadly misinterpreted, even by the most enlightened of humans. So the Director of Pastimes set up a roster, with groups of ten mice at a time taking off from Mouse Hall at five-minute intervals, each group to observe Miss Megan for five minutes precisely.

It worked fine for the first six hundred mice, but at two in the morning Megan stirred. She looked around the room by the dim light that still came from the fireplace and she would have drifted back to sleep if one of the tapestries hadn't moved. It was the scariest of them, one that showed a grinning satyr, half man and half horse, its spear raised in a fierce attack against a terrified stag—frozen in time, until now, when the creature seemed to *move* in Megan's direction, its eyes looking straight at her, its spear aimed at her heart.

When Trey had first made Contact last year, he had been afraid that Megan would scream at the sight of a mouse on her pillow. Sometimes he'd imagined what it might have sounded like if she'd really let loose. But never in his imagination was her scream as loud as the one she came out with now. He and Julia both leapt up from their sleeping positions in a wild scramble, ready for battle, peering around for whatever was endangering their human.

Joey came charging in from the next room to save Megan from wild boars or satyrs or anything else. He switched on the light so that now they could both watch as ten mice shuffled out from behind the tapestry, getting a much better view of Miss Megan than the previous groups, a view that actually had Miss Megan sitting up in bed and laughing.

One of the mice sheepishly explained in MSL why they were there, but Trey didn't translate. No point telling Megan about the roster for gazing at her, because she got quite embarrassed sometimes when mice treated her like a superstar.

Instead he said, "It's the beastie patrol. They take turns all night to make sure you're safe."

And with that, Megan could go back to sleep.

Breakfast at Buckford Hall was duke free, but the absence of the duke was more than made up for by the abundance of food, ranging from regular old bacon and eggs to fried tomatoes and kippers, and from kippers to kidneys and something called kedgeree, which seemed to be fishy.

Even without kippers, kidneys or kedgeree, Megan ate far too much for what happened later. While Jake and her mom could enjoy the luxury of a day with nothing they had to do, a day of total vacation before the rain forest experts arrived, Megan and Joey had to face The Ride.

It would not have been so bad if it had been just them and the groom. He was waiting for them in the stable yard, a short man in a tweedy jacket.

"You kids going to be all right then?" he asked, looking at them a bit dubiously because they were wearing jeans and their regular jackets, with one of Megan's pockets bulging slightly because Julia had come along for the adventure. Megan had invited Trey, but he turned the offer down.

"Oh shoot," he'd told Megan. "Can't make it today. What a pity. Another time, okay? Another time when you're on top of a really stupid mammal who has the power to pitch you off at any moment so that you land on, oh, I don't know, maybe on the pocket of your jacket?"

"There's no way I'd squash you!" Megan had said. But Trey did have a real excuse to stay out of danger. The Brigadier had asked all three talking mice to report for duty in Mouse Hall. With only about eight fully qualified talking mice in the world, most clans never get to meet even one. The presence of three was too much for the Brigadier to pass up, so he had arranged for what he called a "conversation."

Trey would tell the story of The Night when he first made

contact with Megan. Sir Quentin would give them a foretaste of his ode for the Megan Day gala, and Ken had a huge repertoire of limericks with rather dirty last lines.

So it was only Julia in Megan's pocket when the groom introduced her and Joey to a pudgy girl of about nine in just the right sort of jodhpurs, flicking just the right sort of whip against her shiny boots, with blond braids sticking out below just the right sort of hat.

"Miss Olivia's coming with us," said the groom. "Miss Olivia Peabody."

"Oh, is it your dad who . . ." Megan began, but for a moment couldn't think of a way to describe what Mr. Peabody did, except to freak out when he found mice in his shoes.

"That's who she is, all right," said the groom. "It's her pa what really runs this place now, so I have to mind my Ps and Qs when Miss Olivia's around, don't I, miss?"

He grinned to show he was joking, but the girl didn't smile. She looked as if she was not happy, not happy at all, to be riding with kids so improperly dressed.

chapter fourteen

The groom led three ponies one by one to the mounting block in the middle of the yard.

Olivia's pony was calm and round, and so was Joey's, in a slightly larger size. But when it came to Megan's turn, she was alarmed to find that her pony was far more athletic than the others, and seemed eager to take off without bothering to wait for anyone to mount.

"Easy there, Prince," said the groom, standing on the other side of the pony to stabilize him. "He's a bit of a handful, but I'm sure you'll manage, because that's the word I got from His Grace. That you've ridden a lot."

Too late, Megan realized that this was one of those moments in life when you should absolutely say something to clear up a misunderstanding before it kills you. At the very least, she should have mentioned that the animal she'd ridden in the past wasn't 100 percent horse. But she saw Olivia gazing over at her and said nothing. And when Prince stopped tap-dancing just long enough for her to climb on, then scooted straight backward, it did feel familiar for a moment, because backward was Charlie's favorite direction too. Couldn't be so different, could it?

Well, yes, actually, it could. Just the difference between an eighteen-wheeler and a sports car. Just the difference between a lawn mower and a jet plane.

Prince behaved well enough for the first mile or so as the ponies walked behind the groom, though Megan could feel the jittery power that was bottled up beneath her. The trail took them through deep beech woods, most of the leaves now lying soft and spongy on the ground, their sweet autumn scent mingling deliciously with the smell of horse. It was the sort of forest where you could expect Robin Hood to swing down from a branch, or antlers to appear around tree trunks, or boars to come charging at you.

As they headed deeper into the wood, Megan began to relax. She even had time to plan how she'd tell Uncle Fred about this ride, because Prince felt calmer now, as if he was appreciating the stillness of the trees, the muffled clip-clop of hooves on the soft path, the smell of the damp ground. Megan even reached out to pat his neck. Nice pony. Good pony.

Was that her mistake, that little pat? The groom had just reached a fork in the path and turned left, with Olivia right behind him. But something seemed to flip a switch in Prince, to pitch him into a full gallop as he veered away from the group and headed down the other path, the one to the right.

Megan tried pulling on the reins to apply the brakes, but that didn't seem to work, and anyway she soon needed both hands to cling to the saddle, bending low in case Prince found a branch to duck under so he could scrape the load off his back.

The only good thing was the sound of hoofbeats behind her. That must be the groom, right? Ready to get to the front somehow and grab the reins? But when Megan dared to glance

behind her she saw it was Joey, his fat pony gasping for air but still determined to keep up with Prince. Joey, like Megan, was holding tight to the saddle, his eyes wide with the same look that he'd get when he maneuvered his skateboard into an impossible position.

He was *enjoying* this? When Prince was doing his best to kill them both?

No one killed anyone, as it turned out. The forest path came out into the open where an outcropping of smooth rocks guarded a small cliff above a little river, and beyond it, across a narrow bridge, the grounds of Buckford Hall.

Prince paused as if to weigh the choice between a steep slide down to the river and a U-turn back to the woods. That moment of indecision gave Megan time to slide off, holding tight to the reins.

Joey's pony lumbered up beside her.

"That was so cool," he said.

Megan felt shaky all over as she stood in front of Prince, looking him in the eyes as if she could read his mind. If mice were so brilliant, wouldn't it make sense that other mammals had at least a fraction of their intelligence? That somewhere inside this beast there was a brain that could be reasoned with?

But Prince just bared his teeth and tossed his head, his ears laid back in the sign that in mules, at least, means, "Human—you're going DOWN."

There was a wriggling against Megan's side as Julia climbed out of her pocket and up onto her shoulder and made signs to the pony that Megan knew to be very rude. Understandable from a mouse who'd been pitched from a gently swaying ride into a headlong rush that felt as if it could only end in disaster—the disaster of being in the wrong pocket at the wrong time.

Joey was still on top of his pony, so he had a great view of the Buckford Hall grounds laid out beneath them.

"Look," he said. "That maze."

Megan peered between two rocks and saw that a dense square of neatly clipped evergreens was indeed a maze. And now they watched Jake and Susie emerging from it, their arms around each other. Megan wanted to call out—maybe pretend they'd ridden to this bluff on purpose, for the view. But at that moment the groom thundered up on his massive horse, a very unhappy Olivia behind him whining, "Why do we have to go back? It's not fair. Why can't we go to Potts Hill? You promised!"

His back to her, the groom rolled his eyes as he fished a leading rein out of his saddlebag and clipped it to Prince's bridle for the long, slow walk back to the stables.

. . . .

Megan and Joey came back into the huge house through a door that must be close to the kitchen, because they could hear the clanking of pots and pans. A man in jeans was sauntering in their direction.

"'Ello there, guys!" he said.

"Er?" said Joey.

"Don't recognize me without me fancy clothes? I'm John, the footman what grabbed your mouse last night. Sir Crispin, was it? How's he doin'? Not too traumatized, I hope."

"It's Sir Quentin," said Megan. She brought Julia out of her pocket, glad that it was so hard to see the difference between male and female mice. "He's just fine. Look."

"But don't look too close," she thought, then almost cracked up because even though Julia couldn't do human expressions she'd managed to look just like Sir Quentin, with the half-closed eyes, the particular angle of the nose, the slow twitch of the whiskers.

"Cute little fella," said John, reaching over to tickle Julia behind the ears. "Never knew they could be pets, regular old house mice like him. Course, this place is crawling with them, like His Grace said. But he don't seem to mind."

"My sort of duke," said Joey, but it was lost in a roar as Mr. Peabody came around the corner.

"John!" he said. "Why aren't you ready? How many times have I told you that we must make a good first impression! They will be here in ten minutes!"

He bustled off toward the front of the house, and John glared at his back.

"We must make a good first impression," he mouthed silently, then out loud, "If you will forgive me, Master Joey and Miss Megan, I will repair to my quarters in order to"—he looked in the direction of Mr. Peabody to make sure he was out of earshot—"to put on that ridiculous outfit so I can help a bunch of women with their luggage. I mean, hello? What bleeding century is this? But a job's a job, right? See you around."

And he sprinted off down the passage.

The door to the sitting room in the South Tower was open. Jake and Susie were standing at the window gazing out over the parkland at the front of the house.

Susie turned around and reached out her arms toward Megan, holding her at a slight distance for a moment so she could check her over.

"No bruises?" she said. "No broken bones?"

"We thought you'd both be covered with mud and dead

leaves," said Jake. "Bits of forest. Or did you just walk around in a paddock?"

"You kidding?" asked Joey. "We galloped almost the whole time."

"Through the forest," said Megan. "We ended up on that cliff. See it? The other side of that river?"

Susie and Jake looked at each other, impressed. But mice, of course, can't tolerate any bending of the truth, unless they have permission to bend it themselves for the good of their Nation or the planet. Julia leapt to the back of a couch and said something urgent to Trey, who'd just got back from his performance in Mouse Hall.

He ran up Megan's arm to whisper in her ear, "She says, you want to come clean?"

So Megan and Joey told their parents (as they would have done anyway, eventually) about the danger of being on a super-fast pony when you can't find the brakes, or on a slower pony who won't let that fast pony out of his sight. About the indignity of being led back to the stable.

"Hey, it was your first try," said Jake. "If you ride every day, by the time we're finished here, you could, like, learn?"

"And if I jump out of this tower every day I could, like, fly?" said Joey.

"No way, huh?" said Jake.

"No way," said Joey.

And "No way," echoed Megan.

Not on a pony that knew best. Not under the scornful eye of Miss Olivia Peabody.

"The guys downstairs warned us about that twist an' twirl," said Ken. "That girl. One of them heard her dad tellin' her that them American kids had some rough edges, and she could show them how to behave like a proper lady and gentleman."

Which felt about as likely as learning to fly, or letting Prince have another shot at killing you.

It was then that Jake noticed the bus, way off in the distance, wending its way up from the parking lot four miles away where all visitors had to leave their cars. They watched as the bus stopped near the row of footmen beside the front door and unloaded a group of women.

"Quilters," guessed Jake.

"You ever seen a quilter?" asked Susie.

"No, but that's what they must look like, right?"

Yes, middle-aged women, not too worried about their appearance, not exactly fashionably dressed. As often happened, the sight of a group of mammals that she knew little about pushed a button in Susie's scientific brain.

"What sort of women take up quilting?" she wondered. "What is the appeal? Is it making something out of nothing? Or is it the spirit of competition, wanting to do it better than the next person? Or mainly an excuse for social interaction?"

Jake grinned. "I think you should find out," he said. "I think the world needs a report on quilter habitat and nutrition and motivation. And aren't you lucky, a whole herd of quilters right here, ready to be studied. You could take Megan along to keep track of the data. Just like in the old days on your island."

Quilter study seemed a good way to fill the last free afternoon before the experts arrived for their Sea-Level meeting. Before they had to start worrying too much about Coconut Man, and whether he'd come, and whether he'd have proof that he owned the forest and could help them save it.

Megan and her mom set off after lunch, when the quilter herd they were stalking would have been fed, which usually makes herds easier to approach.

Megan led the way to where she guessed the quilters would be setting up in one of the meeting rooms at the back of the house—rooms she and Joey had passed on their long trek back from the stables that morning.

It wasn't hard to find the quilter room from the sound of

furniture being moved, as footmen helped set up tables where half-finished quilts were being laid out. As Megan and her mom peered into the room, a woman in a bright pink jacket came over.

"Can I help you?" she asked.

"I'm intrigued by quilting," said Susie. "Do you mind if I ask you some questions?"

The woman didn't look happy at the interruption, giving the shortest possible answers to Susie's questions about quilter evolution (most of them had mothers who quilted) and quilter habitat (they came from all over) and quilter customs (this group got together at least once a year to quilt). Susie was starting on some more searching questions when Megan tugged urgently on her sleeve.

Her mom gave her the "What makes you think I'm finished?" look. And asked a couple more questions before letting Megan pull her down the corridor as the quilter turned away with what could have been an expression of relief.

"What the . . . ?" Susie began when they were safely in the corridor.

"Mom, didn't you *see*?" asked Megan.

"See what?"

"That quilter in the blue skirt? Her legs were really hairy."

Susie put her hand on Megan's shoulder, which usually

meant a lecture was coming. Something that would help Megan be a better human.

"Honey," said Susie. "We're not in Ohio anymore. This is a different culture. Maybe women in England aren't too worried about a little hair on their legs. It's only natural, after all!"

"But Mom!" said Megan. "It was more than just a little hair! And another woman, the one in pink pants. She had huge hands! As big as Uncle Fred's! Oh, and the one in the leopard skin shirt? Her face was stubbly!"

Her mom's hands dropped to her sides, where they hung loose. Then she leaned against the wall for a moment before she turned back to Megan, her expression bleak, because there could be only one explanation.

chapter fifteen

Megan and her mom ran back up the spiral staircase to the sitting room, where Jake and Joey had fallen asleep watching a billiards game on television.

"Wake up," said Susie, shaking Jake's shoulder.

She told him about the hairy legs. Told him about the stubbly face. Told him about the massive hands.

It was Trey who took charge. He jumped out of Megan's pocket and ran to the back of a couch, forcing his mouth into a strange shape that Megan had seen only a few times before. He was giving the mouse whistle, pitched so high that it was inaudible to humans.

There was a soft tremor in the tapestries, and a messenger mouse emerged. And in response to some short, sharp gestures from Trey he turned and ran behind the tapestries to the hole that led to the palace's underpinnings, and the mouse power that lived there.

The humans all collapsed on the two huge couches of the sitting room while they waited to see what explanation—what excuse—the local mice would come up with. Because how could they have let this palace fill up with quilters who could only be Loggocorp spies?

Megan wanted her own mice for comfort, but for once there were none available. Trey was too tense to come near her, walking around with an expression that Megan knew well. When things went wrong, he had a tendency to blame himself, and she guessed that was happening now. Not a good time to pick him up for a cuddle.

Sir Quentin had attached himself to the platoon of mice on duty in the North Tower, where they kept an eye on the duke himself. Ken was spending the afternoon in Mouse Hall, where he now had a big fan club for his limericks.

And where was Julia?

"Trey!" Megan called out. "Have you seen—"

"She's fine," he said, reading her mind. "Julia's fine. Told me she had a plan. Something she had to do."

But without telling Megan? Without a word to her *human*?

. . . .

It was only a few minutes before a mouse with a blue thread around his neck emerged from behind the tapestry, followed by Ken and a bearer-mouse with a Thumbtop strapped to his back.

"Bit of a setback, yeah?" said Ken. "Them quilters being Julius Caesars. Geezers. Who'd have thought? This bloke will sort things out. The Director of Security."

The director started to speak, as Trey translated.

"We were preparing a report for you," the director said. "We had of course realized instantly that those alleged quilters are in fact male, a few of whom are known to MMI5."

"Shouldn't that be MI5?" said Jake. "Military Intelligence, Section 5? The British FBI?"

"*Mouse* MI5," corrected the director. "That's our investigative agency in London that keeps track of human criminals. They do indeed have three or four of these gentlemen, these *quilters*, in their database."

"What were their crimes?" asked Jake.

"Unauthorized access to computer systems," said the director. "In other words, hacking. And planting listening devices. Most of the alleged quilters, however, are junior executives who work for Loggocorp."

"Oh, Jake, what are we going to do!" said Susie in a very

small voice. "That whole sea-level thing didn't fool them for a minute! Let's tell the duke. Then let's leave, right now."

"There is no need for that," said the director, "because you will of course have the upper hand."

"How?" asked Jake.

The director made a small sign for "Smile" and waved for the bearer-mouse to step forward so Jake could peer at the Thumbtop on his back.

"Observe!" he said. "These gentlemen—these *quilters*—did not waste time. They have already installed a number of listening devices."

There was no way, even with their magnifying glasses, that the humans could make out the details on the floor plan that was squashed onto the tiny screen.

"Just a moment," said Jake, and hurried into the bedroom to fetch the connector that the humans kept ready at all times in case they needed to attach a Thumbtop to something with a larger screen.

It took only a minute to bring up the floor plan on the big television set in the corner, a floor plan with flashing lights that showed exactly where tiny microphones or magic video pens had already been planted.

Nothing in this tower. But bugs in the meeting room

labeled "Sea-Level Task Force"? Check. Blue drawing room? Check. Gold salon? Absolutely. Green morning room? You betcha.

Terrible news, yes? So why was Jake grinning?

"What?" asked Susie.

"The director is right," he said. "We absolutely have the upper hand."

"Huh?" said Susie.

"They don't know we know about those microphones," said Jake. "And we have mice. You know what mice say?"

There are many things that mice say, of course, and for a moment the other humans couldn't guess what he meant. But Trey got it immediately.

"There is no disaster," he said, "that we cannot turn to the advantage of ourselves and our Nation."

"Got it in one, Treyzy Weyzy," said Ken, giving Trey a thump on the back that almost sent him flying. "Not as dumb as you look, me old codger."

"We can get all those quilters into a gigantic mousetrap," said Jake.

Megan sneaked a look at her mom to check her mood, and was relieved to see the beginnings of a smile on Susie's face as she said, "A virtual mousetrap."

"Precisely," said Jake. "With false clues in all those micro-phones. Red herrings—like actually talking about rising seas. And our friends in Mouse Hall will let us know just how well those red herrings are working."

"There's one problem," said Susie.

Megan guessed what it could be. "Your guys might not know that much about rising seas?"

"You got it," said her mom. "I'm sure they all know *some-thing* about the problem, but I don't think they could fill up those microphones for long."

"The Big Cheese," said Joey. "Let's ask the Big Cheese."

Right. If ever there was a job for mice, this was it. Some quick research on rising seas by the experts in Cleveland.

"So who's going to ask the Big Cheese to get all those facts for us?" asked Susie. "Trey? Ken?"

"Ken, I think you . . ." Trey began, and—

"That's your job, innit, Treyzy Weyzy?" said Ken at the same time.

"Oh, I see," said Joey. "You're afraid that the boss will blame *you* for letting the place fill up with quilters."

Trey looked at his paws, and Ken found an urgent need to inspect his tail. Megan guessed that, yes, they were afraid they would be blamed, because weren't mice always expected to see disaster coming and head it off before it hurt their humans? Before it hurt the planet?

"I'll go," said Susie. "I'll tell the Big Cheese what we need, and while I'm at it, I'll ask him how on earth he let us be blindsided like this. Where do I go?"

"It's through a trapdoor in a broom closet," said Trey. "Down near the kitchen, but I don't think—"

Susie wasn't waiting for "buts," and Megan could see that the prospect of action, of doing something positive, did wonders for her mood.

"I'll pretend I'm doing research on the staff," said Susie. "Because it must be a dying profession, being in service in these massive homes. Then I could slip away to your broom closet."

"There's a problem, yeah?" said Ken. "It's a bit of a squash down there, for a full-size human. Don't think you'd fit, to be honest. It would have to be one of them shorter ones."

Joey and Megan looked at each other. "How about the short*est*?" he said.

"Hey—" Megan started to object on principle, as she usually did when Joey tried to stick her with the nastiest mousekeeping jobs. But then she remembered her visit to Headquarters when it was in Silicon Valley—how scary that was at first, but how very glad she was to have gone there. And then Jake gave her the final push.

"Probably best if you do it, Megan," he said, "because you get on so well with the Big Cheese."

"I'll help," said Joey. "We'll play hide-and-seek. I'll distract the staff or the servants or whatever they call themselves. Maybe get that John guy to come hunt for you. In the wrong direction."

It took Susie only five minutes to write out the names of the most useful journals—the ones that would be stuffed with facts about rising sea levels.

Before Megan set off she looked for Julia, who would surely love to be in on any videoconference with Headquarters. With maybe a chance to see Curly and Larry. But Julia still wasn't around, so Megan put Trey in one pocket and a flashlight in the other and followed Joey down the stairs.

They made their way to the passage that led to the kitchen area, then stopped a little way from the clatter of pots and pans before Megan sang out, "Count to twenty and I'll hide!"

As Joey counted, she darted past a game larder, where dead pheasants were hanging, past a room full of hunting rifles and finally to the broom closet, where she hurtled in, closed the door, and lifted up the trapdoor that led to the underpinnings of the massive house.

She dropped down to the damp earth, closed the trapdoor above her, and shone her flashlight around the space as Trey climbed out of her pocket.

"There," he said. "In the corner."

And she saw it. The opening of what looked like a tunnel with a ceiling so low that she had to ooch along it on her stomach with her flashlight in her mouth. For a moment she felt those waves of panic that hit when you imagine that a trapdoor has sealed itself behind you, or an earthquake is about to crumble a massive palace over your head.

"Hang in there," called Trey, who'd been walking ahead. "I see daylight."

With a few more ooches, Megan found herself in Mouse Hall, lit now by the rays of a late sun squeezing their way through a ventilation grille, with motes of dust dancing in the beams. Here there was room to sit up and face the group of mice waiting for her, a Thumbtop in front of them. They had already made the connection with Cleveland, because there was the Big Cheese himself on the tiny screen.

"Oh sir," said Megan. "We could really use your help. They know we're here. Loggocorp knows we're here."

She told him about the quilters. Told him about the need to fill Loggocorp's microphones with facts about rising seas. Then she added her mom's question. How did mice let their humans be blindsided? Let them walk into a trap?

What had Megan expected? The twitch of the whiskers that meant a storm was coming? Rage at the British mice who had failed to warn his humans? An apology, because this safe haven had turned out to be anything but?

What she got was only a slight smile.

"With regard to the infestation of Buckford Hall by Loggocorp spies," he said, "although mice are powerful, not all human actions are under our control! However, I will of course provide you with a full explanation of how the infestation came about in due course."

"But . . ." Megan began, because she guessed that her mom would like at least a partial explanation right now.

"But you may tell your parents that they need not worry," said the Big Cheese, with something in his gestures that plainly meant that the topic of Loggocorp spies was now closed. "The original plan is still in place, and the representative of Coconut Man's family will make contact as planned, before the end of the week."

"And the research?" Megan prompted.

"That will be provided overnight," said the Big Cheese, "so the experts can talk with confidence on the subject of rising seas. Fortunately, most of the scientists in the group are known to have some concern about the oceans, so there is a good chance that Loggocorp will accept that their interest is real. However, such is not the case with President Pindoran, whose presence would of course immediately reveal the group's connection with Marisco and its rain forest. It would therefore be best if no president were in attendance."

"But sir," said Megan, "I don't think my mom can tell him not to come. Our phones and computers don't work here."

"Did I say that the gentleman should not attend?" asked the Big Cheese. He was looking at Megan with the sort of triumphant expression that she was quite used to by now, the one that means, "Don't you know how lucky you are to have mice doing your thinking for you?"

"We took the precaution of booking his room under the name of Dr. Patel, a scientist from Fiji. That nation comprises hundreds of islands, many of them in danger from rising sea levels. Now, please let me talk to a member of the Buckford

Hall IT team so I can arrange the delivery of the research you require."

An IT mouse stepped forward, and Megan sat back from the Thumbtop, watching the signs of MSL shooting back and forth. She could hear feet thundering above her head, with shouts from maybe a footman, maybe a maid or two, helping Joey to hunt. She looked at her watch. Only three minutes until the time they'd arranged for Joey to do his distracting in the other direction, making it safe for her to emerge.

The IT mouse had received his instructions, and the Big Cheese had one last word for Megan.

"You will find the information on rising seas tomorrow morning in the storeroom adjacent to the main office," he said. "The transformation of President Pindoran into Dr. Patel I leave to you."

The Big Cheese's image had just faded away when Megan jumped, which wasn't good in that confined space, because her head hit a beam. A mouse had run up her arm. If the truth be told, strange mice still carried an EEEEK factor for the five Humans Who Knew. Megan froze, which prompted the mouse to run down her arm again and stand in front of her, pointing to its ear. Two dots. Julia. And was that a wisp of cobweb on her, as if she'd been exploring the maze of tunnels in this place?

"Where've you *been*?" Megan whispered a bit crossly.

It wasn't as if she *owned* her mice. She couldn't tell them what to do. But still, when one of them just took off like that without telling her . . . She couldn't help glaring now, and Julia's ears drooped as if she felt guilty. Then she made a couple of tentative gestures. The sign for "Mouse" (paws reach up to ears). Then a paw at about half mouse height. Young mice. Hanging out with young mice? Some more signs that Megan didn't recognize.

She glanced at Trey. Help needed here!

He grinned at her and whispered, "You don't want to know." Then he did a pirouette. Was he in a great mood because of something Julia had said? Or because his own boss seemed to be in charge again, all the way from Cleveland?

Trey didn't explain, and it was time for Megan to go, with the two mice walking ahead of her for the slow ooching journey out of Mouse Hall. When they reached the space under the trapdoor, Megan waited until the thunder of feet and the happy hunting sounds faded off into the middle distance. Then she pushed up through the trapdoor, left the broom closet and sang out, "Na na, na na na, you never found me!" She sprinted for the spiral staircase, because of course she couldn't let Joey and the servants find her. Not with her jeans coated in dust and the cobwebs of centuries making her hair look almost gray.

chapter sixteen

E arly the next morning Megan and Joey headed for the storeroom where mice had stashed the seventy-five pages that they had printed up in the night, downloaded by way of Mr. Peabody's computer. Megan kept watch while Joey darted into the room to grab the stack of paper, and to help himself to a file folder and a marker pen.

Shortly before eleven, Julia spotted the van making its way up from the road—the van that had collected the rain forest experts from their supersecret hotel near London Airport.

The four humans set off on the long walk through the majestic rooms that led to the front door. They couldn't say much on the way, of course, because they knew that some of the furniture was listening, and some of the pictures of mythological weirdos and old dukes and their favorite hunting dogs had their ears wide open.

A posse of footmen was waiting at the front portico, while Mr. Peabody went up and down the line checking that their livery was on straight. And there was Olivia, now wearing a frilly pink dress.

When the van stopped and a footman leapt forward to slide open its door, Megan held up the file folder sign she and Joey had made:

WELCOME
SEA-LEVEL
TASK FORCE

Megan's mom had met all the experts before at conferences, and as they came up to greet her, or hug her, or kiss her cheek, she whispered, "Sea level," to Sir Brian, and to Heinrich the zoologist from Germany, and to Pierre the botanist from France, and to Laura the lemur lady from Australia, and to Martin the climatologist from Ghana.

Last out of the van was a tall man in a light-colored suit who needed more than a change of subject for the meeting. He needed a new identity.

"Dr. Patel!" said Susie, sweeping down on him. "So glad you could make it, because your problems in Fiji are so troubling! How much of your country is in danger from rising sea levels?"

From where she was standing, Megan could see her mom's right eye, which was winking nonstop as she gazed into the ex-president's face. First that face gazed back with an expression that was totally blank, but then the new Dr. Patel got it.

"Fiji has indeed hundreds of islands," he said. He spoke English with great care, as if each syllable were a jewel to be polished in his mouth before he'd let it out. "And nearly all of them are threatened."

He turned back to the van, because emerging from the backseat was a total distraction from sea levels, rain forests, and fake scientists from Fiji. It was a boy. Who'd said anything about a boy? But there he was, grabbing the president's hand. A boy of about six, wearing an English school uniform.

"I hope you don't mind that I brought my son Chaz," said the ex-president. "He is currently living with a relative of mine in London, where he attends an English school."

"We are delighted to have your little chap as our guest, Dr. Patel," said Mr. Peabody. "My daughter will entertain him while you are at your meetings. Now, if your party would care to gather in the blue drawing room, morning coffee will be served."

Except for one problem.

The blue drawing room was on the mouse map. There was one voice-activated microphone behind the Louis the Fourteenth credenza, just below the portrait of a duke's favorite dog. Another was tucked behind a picture of the tenth duke at the age of three, and the fake snuff box on an eighteenth-century desk housed a motion-activated video camera.

"Thank you," said Megan's mom, "but we'd rather start off in our suite, so could you please arrange for coffee to be brought up there? I mean, you *have* to see our place," she said to Sir Brian. "It's a hoot."

She led the parade back toward the spiral staircase of the South Tower. A parade with Olivia tagging along, talking to Chaz.

Megan hung back to listen.

"You don't have to go with the grown-ups," Olivia was saying. "You can come and play with me. I have some toys in my room and you can have lunch with me and then we can play hide-and-seek. Would you like that, Chazzy?"

Trey gave Megan a sharp jab from her pocket, meaning no way they should let the kid out of their sight, because who knew what he might say about his father's real job, and real name, and real purpose for being here?

The procession had reached the bottom of the spiral staircase when Megan took control. She grabbed Chaz's hand and said, "Thanks, Olivia," meaning, "You can get lost now."

For a moment Olivia clutched at Chaz's other hand, saying, "But my daddy said! He said I should look after him."

"Later," said Megan, and led Chaz up the spiral stairs. But not before Olivia had sung out, "She's weird, Chaz. She's not normal. One of the footmen told me. She has a *mouse* and it's not like a pet mouse. It's a *pest*."

A footman brought trays of coffee and cookies to the South Tower. As soon as he had gone, all eyes turned accusingly on Susie and Jake.

"For what purpose," asked Martin, the climatologist from Ghana, "must we hide our true reason for being here?"

"Changing the topic of our meeting, changing my name," said President Pindoran. "That does not bode well."

"After all our efforts to preserve secrecy," said Heinrich the zoologist, putting down his cup as if it too might be spying on him. "After all those cat-and-mouse games that you said would keep us safe. How can this be?"

"Susie, it is well known that you have excellent contacts," said Sir Brian. "You are able to discover facts about climate deniers, for example, that elude the rest of us. But now, have even you been bamboozled?"

"Yes," admitted Susie. "Bamboozled is about right. Jake?"

Jake stood up to face the group, his back to the fireplace. He told the group about quilters. Quilters with big hands and stubbly faces. Quilters with hair in places where it doesn't usually grow on a quilter.

"We double-checked this room," he continued, "and here, it is safe to talk. But we have a strong suspicion that Loggocorp has planted listening devices in many other corners of this house."

The experts exploded, in different ways. Pierre and Heinrich said things in French and German that sounded rude. Martin the climatologist shook his head sadly, and Laura the lemur lady flapped her hands as if that could make the unpleasant facts go away.

Ex-President Pindoran reached for his son. "I had thought England to be so safe," he said. "That is why I sent Chaz to live in London, while the generals have our own country in such turmoil."

"Let's just leave!" said Sir Brian. "Let's just tell that Peabody chap to bring back our van so we can go somewhere else!"

"We can't leave," said Susie. "This is where we'll meet the person from Coconut Man's family. I got a message. He'll meet us here today or tomorrow."

Chaz's eyes were huge.

"Does Coconut Man have a family?" he asked.

His father gave him a hug.

"The legend of Coconut Man is strong in my country," he explained. "The children believe that he brings them gifts, much like your Santa Claus."

"Well, his descendants can give the children the best gift of all," said Laura, smiling at Chaz. "They can leave the forest intact, so the lemurs can thrive."

"But with this house full of spies . . ." Heinrich objected.

"We have the advantage, don't you see!" said Jake. "That's where the rising seas come in. You can bamboozle these Loggocorp people."

"Lull them to sleep," said Susie.

"Bore them to death," said Jake. "Feed their microphones with red herrings. Nothing except facts about the ocean. With luck, they'll give up and go away."

Megan noticed that for the first time, a few smiles were showing.

"Well, it's worth a shot," said Sir Brian.

Martin the climatologist made the obvious objection. "Hours and hours of talk about sea levels?" he asked. "Hands up anyone who feels qualified to do that!"

No hands went up, but they didn't have to, of course.

"We've thought of that," said Susie. "Joey?"

Joey reached under a seat cushion where he'd hidden the stack of research papers that had come overnight from Cleveland, and handed them to Susie.

"Here are your red herrings," she said. "All the herrings that Loggocorp can possibly digest. We can take turns reading these papers aloud in our conference room, which we're sure is bugged. Then we can come back here to work on the real presentation for Coconut Man's descendant."

Laura had gotten up to look through the window.

"We could talk freely outside," she said, "in these lovely, lovely gardens."

"Or not," said ex-President Pindoran, joining her at the window.

Chaz ran over to look.

"It's some ladies," he said.

"Very special ladies," said the president, putting his hands on Chaz's shoulders. "Come and see, everybody."

A group of quilters was making its way to the gazebo, an

elegant structure like a little bandstand in the middle of the smooth expanse of lawn. Some of them seemed to be working on their disguise a bit harder than necessary, as if this whole quilter caper was hilarious. A tall one was taking tiny steps, occasionally putting up a hand to pat carefully curled gray hair. Two were swaying their hips like caricatures of runway models, and some of the others fell about laughing, looking far more like young men than the middle-aged women they were supposed to be.

The woman in the pink jacket—the only real woman, as far as Megan could tell—ran from one to the other, giving them sharp taps to bring them back into line, looking anxiously for watchers at the palace windows while the actual watchers drew back.

"Clowns!" said Heinrich the zoologist.

"Yes, but dangerous clowns," said the ex-president. "Dangerous to my country."

When they reached the gazebo, the quilters swarmed all over it, some standing in clumps to mask what might be going on behind them.

"Bet they're planting microphones," guessed Jake. "Probably with sticky backs, so they can put them anywhere, like under those seats."

"One more habitat for red herrings, don't you think?" said Sir Brian.

"An excellent place for fish to swim," said Pierre.

"Fishes?" said Chaz, with a laugh. "Fishes can't swim in that little house!"

Susie bent down to give him a hug.

"It's just a figure of speech," she said. "Megan? Can you explain figures of speech? And maybe play with Chaz while our friends work on the proposal for the Coconut guy?"

"Which had better be good," said Heinrich grimly.

"Very, very good," said Pierre, gazing down at the lawn. "Now we know what we are up against."

Yes, in a palace full of quilters who could offer millions of dollars for the rights to the forest, the proposal to save it would have to be very good indeed.

chapter seventeen

Megan hadn't expected that her role in saving the rain forest would involve babysitting. Wouldn't it be better if Joey played with Chaz, teaching him boy stuff like sliding into third base? So she could listen to these great scientists? But Joey had sat down next to his dad as if he were part of the planning group, and was definitely avoiding her eye.

Megan sighed, while Chaz looked up at her expectantly. She grinned at him. It was hard not to, because he was exceptionally cute. But what did six-year-old boys like to do? Board games? Coloring? Hide-and-seek?

There were no board games in this royal room. No nice fat boxes of crayons. And hide-and-seek? No way she could let Chaz loose in the palace, stuffed as it was with quilters.

It was Chaz who came up with a suggestion.

"That girl said you have a mouse," he said.

"I do," she said. With a silent apology to Trey, Megan fished him out of her pocket.

"Cool," said Chaz. "Can I hold him?"

All mice know that next to the cat and birds of prey, the most dangerous creature on the planet is the human male between the ages of two and about fifteen. And when Chaz reached out, hoping to pluck the mouse out of Megan's hand, Trey threw her an anguished look that meant "Communication needed."

"This is a very special mouse," she said. "I think he wants to tell me something."

"Mice can't talk!" said Chaz with a broad grin, as she held Trey up to her face.

"Make it a game," he whispered. "Let me go, then tell him to whistle 'God Save the Queen.' It's the same tune as 'My Country, 'Tis of Thee.' Remember that one?"

For the first time in the history of the world a mouse hummed to a human.

"Got it," said Megan. "Okay, Chaz, I'm going to show you one of Mousie's tricks. He'll go hide, then all you have to do is whistle 'God Save the Queen' and he'll come running back. You know how that goes, right?"

She whistled the first few bars of "My Country, 'Tis of Thee."

"Course I know it," said Chaz, as Trey scampered off and vanished behind a tapestry. "We sing it every day at school."

He puckered up his lips, but whistling wasn't going to happen, so he sang the tune instead. And a mouse came running back. Not the familiar mouse with a notch missing from his ear where a rat had once chomped it, but a British mouse responding briskly, as they all do, to their national anthem.

It was brilliant. A mouse game that could keep Chaz happy indefinitely, as mouse after mouse sprinted for the tapestry and mouse after mouse came back when he sang out the first bars of their song.

Now Megan was free to listen as the group began work on the presentation they would make when the person from Coconut Man's family appeared. The presentation that could save the rain forest.

It was after lunch that the first red herrings swam into quilters' ears.

The rain forest experts were gathered around the table in their designated meeting room, bristling though it was with hidden microphones. Megan and Joey sat in a corner of the room with Chaz, who was busy playing games on a tablet that one of the experts had loaned to him.

The plan worked beautifully. What reached the ears of the quilters was purest herring, as the experts took turns reading journal articles on the rising seas.

Herring One, for example, consisted of facts and figures about the rate of ice melt in Greenland and the Antarctic, and its effect on coastal cities. Herring Two focused on the expansion of water as it warms. Herring Three was about the loss of farmland, as higher tides and storm surges left layers of salt behind.

And Megan could imagine quilters' heads spinning, because this was surely not what they expected.

The quilters couldn't know, of course, what the rain forest experts were actually doing while their parade of ocean facts marched by. The whiteboard in the conference room was soon covered with rain forest facts and suggestions for the rain forest's future, like setting up a foundation that would be run by ex-President Pindoran. Hiring Mariscans to guard the forest and protect the lemurs. Building a lab on the edge of the forest so researchers could study plants that might hold the key to new medicines. Providing an educational center where people from all over the world could learn the importance of keeping the wilderness intact.

At one point Megan felt Trey climb out of her pocket as he went off to check with the central command post in Mouse Hall. When he came back, he worked his way up to her ear to whisper, "It's working! The quilters are totally flummoxed. Gobsmacked. Yelling at each other. One of them just used Mr. Peabody's phone to call someone in London. He said it looked like this group wasn't the one they'd expected after all!"

At about four o'clock, Heinrich carefully rubbed all evidence of rain forest planning from the chalkboard. Sir Brian stood up and yawned loudly.

"It is a little stuffy in here, and the weather is fine," he said. "A little exercise will wake us up. I suggest that we stroll through these magnificent grounds while we discuss the next topic: protecting coastal cities."

The first stop on that stroll was the gazebo, where two experts reminded each other of the massive steel walls that spring into place to protect Dutch cities from storms, and another mentioned the barriers that keep the River Thames out of the London streets. Good herrings for the microphones under the seats.

Then it was time for the truth stroll, and the group set off across the huge lawn while they discussed the real ideas that had been proposed on the whiteboard inside.

Megan and Joey missed that bit. Chaz was about to explode with the need to run around, and Susie had asked them to play with him. They chased him, pretending he was hard to catch, until he turned out to be *really* hard to catch, diving into the duke's maze. When Megan and Joey arrived at the entrance, all they could hear was a distant "You can't find me!"

Which was followed in a few seconds by a wail. "I'm lost! Come and get me!"

"Let's just leave him," said Joey.

"We can't," said Megan. Soft whimpering sounds were now emerging from deep in the maze.

"Just sit down and wait, Chaz," Megan called. "We're coming."

They both set off into the maze, with Joey taking the first left and Megan the first right, but it soon became plain that it would be far easier to get totally lost than to find a small boy stuck somewhere in the middle. So they traced their way back to the opening.

"We could fetch his dad," suggested Joey. "And the others. They could all hold hands so no one gets lost."

Which looked like the last thing the clump of experts wanted to do now, as they were heading off to the farthest point on the lawn, with Laura the lemur lady walking backward in front of them, waving her arms excitedly to make her point.

"You guys," said Trey, climbing out of Megan's pocket.

"What?" asked Joey.

Trey gave him the exasperated look that mice use when humans think they can do things that are plainly better left to another species.

"Give us two minutes to map the maze," said Trey. "Then have him sing 'God Save the 'Tis of Thee,' or 'My Country the Queen.' Whatever."

The mapping didn't take long. After centuries of living in dark labyrinths under houses and palaces, mice have developed an extraordinary sense of geography, like a built-in GPS. Julia took the left side of the maze, running straight through its dense yew hedges and memorizing its turns and dead ends, while Trey took the right.

Megan checked her watch. By now the two mice must be close to the center, so she called out, "Sing 'God Save the Queen,' Chaz. And someone you know will lead you out."

She expected, of course, a joyous cry of "Mousie," but that's not what came from the depths of the maze. Instead it was "God save the . . . Oh, hallo. Have you come to rescue me? Are you a good witch or something?"

chapter eighteen

good *witch*? For a second Megan wondered if there was some deep secret her mice had kept from her. All their talk about how you don't need magic when you have mice—was that just to make her think they *couldn't* do magic? When secretly they knew how to transform themselves into witches?

But the voice she heard next was very human.

"Hold my hand, sonny, and I'll lead you out," it said, "even though I'm not exactly a witch!"

Megan and Joey watched the dark entrance of the maze until a woman emerged leading Chaz—a couple of tears still making wet lines on his cheeks. He broke away and ran to Megan, giving her a hug.

Megan made herself smile at the woman, who smiled back and said, "So we meet again," because this was the quilter

Megan and her mom had talked to earlier. The one in a bright pink jacket. The one who was an actual woman.

"Such a dear little boy," she said, and headed back toward the big house. Chaz ran off to join his father, as the experts made the turn at the far end of the huge lawn and started back toward the maze.

Joey ran off too, following Chaz, but Megan was in no hurry to go anywhere. She'd just been hit by a huge wave of jet lag and all she wanted to do was to lie down, to be alone, to take a nap on the grass, dry and warm in the soft October sun. She gazed up at the clouds, which looked like the map of Lake Erie . . . mice . . . herrings.

Her eyes were closed and she was almost asleep when she felt Trey coming back from the maze, nesting gently against her neck. But no one could have slept through the arrival of Julia, who jumped onto Megan's ankle, ran all the way along her body to pull on an ear, then started poking at Trey who said, "Hey, cut it out. What the . . . ? Uh-oh."

"What?" said Megan, abandoning all thoughts of a nap. "What do you mean, 'Uh-oh'?"

She sat up, and Julia stood in front of her, launching a torrent of MSL, her gestures faster than any Megan had seen her make before. Trey translated: it was the story of what Julia had been doing with those young mice yesterday afternoon. She didn't want to tell Megan at first, because in a mild way she'd been doing harm to a human, which was a violation of the Treaty Between the Species—the part that read:

* Mice will never hurt humans.

But now it all came out.

When Megan and Joey had returned to the South Tower after the ride yesterday, Julia had slipped away behind the tapestry and down through the walls to Mouse Hall. There, she had asked some young girl mice to lead her to Olivia's room because she *hated* the way Olivia had sneered at Megan and Joey that morning. Nobody, no human alive, was allowed to treat Megan like that. To imply that Megan wasn't properly dressed. Or that she couldn't properly ride. Or that she wasn't properly brought up. Whatever.

As Julia had suspected, the girl mice often visited Olivia's room, curious about what young human females read, and write, and put up on their walls. Two of the mice led Julia up there. Even better, they helped with one of the more common revenge tricks that mice play on humans—tying unmatched shoes together in a knot that few humans can unpick.

When that business was done, Julia took a moment to look around. Two things about the room interested her. One was the magnificent quilt on the bed. And the other?

Trey had reached this part of the translation when he stopped and gazed at Julia in silence for a moment before he turned to Megan.

"Better save this for when your mom can hear it," he said. "It's serious stuff."

The experts had almost finished their circumnavigation of the lawn, so it didn't take Megan long to cut the three Humans Who Knew out of the pack.

"Can't it wait?" Susie asked. "We were just deciding what point to make first when son of Coconut Man shows up, or great-great-grandson—whatever."

She was looking more cheerful than she had for weeks, and Megan hated to squelch her good mood.

"Sit," she said. "Julia has something very important to tell us."

The humans sat on the grass with their backs to the experts as Trey translated the rest of Julia's story.

There was a photograph on Olivia's dresser. A picture of a woman working on the quilt that was now on Olivia's bed, with the message, "For darling Olivia. From Auntie Flo."

"And it was the same woman," Julia continued. "The quilter who was in the maze, where she was probably planting a bug."

"She's the one we talked to yesterday, Mom," said Megan. "The real woman."

"*That* quilter?" exclaimed Susie, her voice squeaky. "Olivia's *aunt* is a quilter? So the *Peabody* family's involved in this? That must be how Loggocorp knew we were here—from Peabody. But what's *his* connection to Loggocorp?"

Joey's imagination was off and running. "Maybe Loggocorp wants to cut down all the duke's trees." He waved at the beech woods, marching up to the creek that bordered the huge lawn. "And it's Peabody's job to get the duke to sell them."

"That would be too much of a coincidence, don't you think?" said Jake. "If Loggocorp just happened to have an ally here?"

"Maybe," said Susie. "But he's here! For whatever reason. That's what we have to deal with. And maybe it's not just him. Maybe all those footmen are working for Loggocorp too. All those maids."

"We'd better tell the duke," said Jake. "Tell him his palace is riddled with spies."

"Hey, maybe he's already in on it too," said Joey. "Maybe he's being paid off by Loggocorp. He needs money, remember, to keep up this place. Maybe that was his own red herring, when he said he was worried about climate change."

That brought everyone up short. Megan gazed at the huge house. All those windows gazing back, and behind each one a spy? Including those windows on the far right, the ones in the North Tower?

"We'll ask Sir Quentin," said Trey. "He's on watch in the duke's apartment."

"D'you think Sir Quentin would notice anything?" said Joey. "D'you think he'd ever be suspicious of his precious duke?"

Trey gave him a very sharp look. "Five is a mouse," he said curtly.

Yes, and mouse instincts always take precedence over behavior that a mouse has learned. In a battle between Sir Quentin and the underlying mouse, the basic mouse would come out on top, even if it meant betraying a duke.

"I won't tell the others about the Peabodys," said Susie. "It would be hard to explain how we knew, without the mouse part. I'll take everyone back to our room as if nothing has happened. We'll keep working on that presentation and hope the Coconut guy shows up *soon*, so we can get out of here."

A couple of maids delivered trays of tea with crumpets and Marmite sandwiches to the South Tower, but there was one problem (besides the Marmite, which got Pierre launched on a long speech on how only the British would eat that sludge left over from the process of brewing beer).

The problem was Chaz. He'd recovered enough from his adventure in the maze to be bored out of his skull. He kept tugging at his father's knee, or elbow, and whining, "There's nothing to *do*." A classic six-year-old pain in the butt.

"Megan?" called out Susie. "You and Joey. Can you . . . ?"

Megan sighed, because from the scowl on Chaz's face, it would require more than a few rounds of "My Country, 'Tis of Thee" to entertain him.

"We could take him off to explore," she said, picking up her jacket and trailing it behind the couch where Julia and Trey had been hiding, so they could climb into pockets.

"An excellent idea," said the ex-president. "But I suggest that you not go outdoors, my son, so that no maze can suck you in."

It was a bit like a maze indoors too, after they'd marched Chaz through the tourist part of the house, answering his questions—more or less—about the things that were happening in some of the stranger pictures.

Once they reached the last of the rooms with red velvet ropes—a pink parlor for the use of past duchesses—there was a decision to make. Whether to turn back the way they had come or to make a circle, threading their way back through narrow passages that led past the kitchen. Then past the quilters.

"Better go straight back," said Megan, whispering because who knew what piece of furniture, what picture, might be listening?

"Oh, come on," whispered Joey. "We have to act natural, remember? We don't suspect a thing!"

So they took Chaz through the back part of the house, past the kitchen and the servants' hall, where a clinking of cups suggested that it was teatime there too. Then on past the game larder with its rows of dead pheasants, past the room full of guns, past the broom closet that hid the entrance to Mouse Hall.

And straight into disaster.

It came in the form of Aunt Flo, emerging from the quilters' room. She broke out a huge smile at the sight of Chaz.

"Hallo, my friend!" she said. "I think I see a little boy who would like some chocolate cake."

chapter Nineteen

unt Flo grabbed Chaz's hand and marched him briskly back the way they had come. Megan and Joey could only follow them into a room where people in various uniforms and liveries were sitting around a long table drinking tea. Yes, there was chocolate cake. There was also Olivia, eating a small and ladylike piece of it.

"Hello, guys," said John the footman. "Didn't fancy those Marmite sandwiches? Can't blame you for that. Here, have some cake."

Megan and Joey looked at each other. It couldn't hurt, could it, sitting down for a few minutes? If they kept Chaz between them, kept him safe?

Except for one thing. Except for the conversation, which was hard to control, especially when a round woman who seemed to be a cook asked, "And what have you been up to this afternoon, little man?"

"Making fishes with my daddy," said Chaz, his mouth full. "Red herrings for the Coconut Man."

Megan and Joey looked at each other, aghast.

"It's a game we play in America," said Joey quickly. "Make the fish and win a coconut."

"It's really fun," said Megan, her fingers crossed to cover the lie. "Someone makes a cardboard fish, which can be any color and any sort of fish—I like it best when it's a trout. A blue trout. One person is the fisherman and that person hides the fish . . ."

She looked around. Most of the people around the table were listening solemnly, with the slight smile English people get when they think Americans are being strange. Except Aunt Flo, who looked as if someone had lit a lightbulb above her head.

"What's that Coconut Man called, Chaz?" she asked.

"That's a secret!" said Chaz. "But I think my daddy knows."

Megan put her hands in her pockets for a quick stroke of Trey and Julia, who had come along for the ride. Should she bring one of them out? Set off enough EEEEKing so everyone would scatter and they could escape and Chaz could do no more damage?

Joey jumped in with his own rescue attempt.

"What are you talking about, Chaz?" he said. "The coconuts' names aren't secret! There's Fred and Harry. And Sarah. That gets you the highest score, remember? When you win the Sarah coconut?"

Yes, the maids and the footmen and the cook were properly fooled. But Aunt Flo was leaning forward as if a new question was coming, and Megan knew that they had to get Chaz out of there *now*. Before he said anything more specific about coconuts in general and the descendants of Coconut Man in particular.

"Look at the time!" she said. "Gotta go now. Bye, everyone, and thanks for the cake."

She grabbed one of Chaz's arms as Joey grabbed the other, and they ran him out of the room, turning south toward their tower and safety.

They'd underestimated Chaz, though. They hadn't gone far when he wriggled free, roaring, "I didn't finish my cake," and sprinted away at top speed. Megan and Joey took off after him, of course, as he headed back toward the servants' hall. But they weren't the ones to stop him.

Chaz had disappeared around a corner, barely ten feet ahead of them, when they heard an awful sort of splat, followed by a wail of pain and a gruff, "I say, old chap, are you all right?"

As Megan and Joey raced around the corner, there was the

duke. His Grace. Billy. Sitting in his wheelchair with Chaz on his knee, howling.

"Rotten show, what?" said the duke. "Poor little fellow. Ran into my wheelchair. Confounded thing has a mind of its own. Couldn't find the brakes."

Chaz had a gash on his knee, and his blood was dripping onto the duke's tweed trousers.

"I'll take him up to my quarters in the North Tower," said the duke. "Would you like that, little man?" He was speaking now in the sort of soft voice people use on babies. "I'll mend your knee and give you a treat, to make up. Would you like some chocky bickies? And some sweeties?"

"We'd better take him back to his dad," said Joey.

"Nonsense!" said the duke. "His father's a busy man, saving the oceans. I'll make his knee as good as new. Come along."

They should have insisted, of course. That was their first big mistake—not insisting. But how do you insist with a duke? In his own palace?

They had to trot to keep up as the duke motored along the passages that led to the North Tower. While they ran, they noticed movement at the back of the wheelchair, and a mouse stuck his head out of the bag hanging there. Sir Quentin? Megan tried to remember the MSL for "Who are you?" but the duke was rolling into an elevator, and she and Joey had to run to get in with him before it groaned its way up to the second floor.

The elevator disgorged them straight into the duke's sitting room, which was furnished with slightly shabby chairs and couches in patterns that did not match, grouped around a fireplace where logs were burning.

Megan tried, one more time.

"We'd really better take Chaz back to . . ."

"What?" said the duke. "And have the little chap bleeding like a stuck pig all over my house? He's not going anywhere until I've patched him up and he's had his chocky bickies."

As the duke rolled into his bathroom to look for a Band-Aid, with Chaz still on his knees, the mouse who'd been riding on the wheelchair jumped onto the coffee table and made a little bow to Megan and Joey. And yes, it was indeed Sir Quentin.

"Welcome to what I almost think of as my own abode," he whispered. "I was outraged when a messenger from Mouse Hall asked me whether His Grace might be in cahoots with the villains under his roof! I have been able to scrutinize His Grace at every turn and can report that in my view he is above suspicion!"

"Good work, Sir Q!" whispered Joey. "So your job here's

kind of done, right? Well, I have another one for you—to take a message to my dad."

He looked over at Megan, who nodded. Yes, some talking mouse should definitely tell their parents where they were and reassure them that Chaz was in good hands.

At the prospect of leaving his duke, Sir Quentin drooped.

"I had been hoping to find further proof exonerating His Grace," he said. "To ensure that not one thread of suspicion should besmirch his good name."

Julia gave him an exasperated look and launched into a burst of MSL.

"She'll go," Trey translated, "because I'd better stick with you guys, just in case. She'll fetch Ken from Mouse Hall and get him to tell your parents."

Julia gave Megan a quick farewell nuzzle and sprinted for the duke's kitchen, because kitchens nearly always have a gap under the counters that leads to the mouse system of trails behind the walls.

And it wasn't until she had gone that Megan's mind clicked onto what Trey had said. He'd better stay with them just in case? In case of what? But before she could ask, the duke emerged from his bathroom with Chaz still on his knee and still bleeding.

"Don't seem to have the right sort of sticky plasters here," said the duke, rolling over to tug on the long bellpull beside his fireplace. As always happened, a human appeared—a footman this time, but one whom Megan didn't recognize. Nor did the duke.

"You're the new chap, what?" he asked.

"I am, Your Grace," said the man, and Megan got the feeling that he hadn't yet been fitted for his permanent footman outfit, because the one he was wearing looked a bit tight.

"Take this little man down to the first-aid room and ask someone to patch up his knee," said the duke. "Then bring him back for his chocky bickies."

"I want Megan to come with me," said Chaz, and she stood up, but the duke waved for her to sit down again.

"I want, I want," he said. "We can't have everything we want in this world. Run along like a good little man while I talk to these young Yanks."

Later, Megan wondered how she and Joey could possibly have let Chaz go like that? But when a duke gives you orders, it's hard to disobey, and she and Joey sat obediently while the duke asked them about America. Was it anything like all those programs on the telly? *The Simpsons*, for example. "Don't suppose your ladies really have blue hair, what?" And the food? What exactly was a milkshake? And a Sloppy Joe? American football, now. He'd seen it once on television.

"Team kept stopping the game for some kind of debate! Never saw such a thing!" he was saying, when Megan finally got the courage to be rude, and stood up.

"If you don't mind, we'd better go and find Chaz," she said.

"I say, time has flown," said the duke. "I wonder what's keeping the little fellow. Perhaps you should check up on him. He'll be in the first-aid room next to the scullery. That's where we patch up the trippers when they trip. I say, that's not a bad joke, what? Trippers tripping? If he's not there, he's probably in the servants' hall with everyone making a big fuss over him. Dear little chap."

Megan and Joey took the elevator downstairs, hoping all was well, hoping they had not been disastrously dumb, letting themselves be cowed by a duke. They ran to the room where the first-aid supplies were kept. Yes, someone had opened a package of Band-Aids and left a tube of ointment on the counter. But no Chaz.

As they hurried toward the servants' hall, a sick feeling in Megan's stomach grew with each step. *Please, please, oh please let Chaz be there,* she thought. *Please, please, oh please let him be sitting at the table, stuffing his face with chocolate cake.*

John the footman was just coming out of the servants' hall, brushing crumbs off his livery. "Hello there! You lookin' for that Chaz? A bit late, ain't you? He's in the hands of the dreaded . . ."—he lowered his voice and crouched, looking furtively over a shoulder—". . . the dreaded Peabody. Fuss about nothing, if you ask me. Wasn't much of a cut, as far as I could see, but Mr. Peabody, he's the only one what's allowed to have a car up here at the house, so he took the kid to the doctor, him and his sister, Flo."

"Wait, wait—Mr. Peabody took him to a *doctor*?" asked Joey. "Which doctor?"

"No, not a witch doctor," said John, laughing. "Just a regular one."

Which made Megan mad. This was so much not the time for jokes. "Joey means where did Mr. Peabody take him?" she asked.

"I don't know, to be honest," said John. "Closest doctors are about five miles away. One in Milford, and another in Shepton."

It was Joey who asked the crucial question. "Did Mr.

Peabody tell Chaz's dad where they were going?" he asked. "Did he tell the . . . Dr. Patel?"

"I think he must have, don't you? But come to think of it, they left in a bit of a rush. Maybe you'd better tell his dad yourself, so he won't worry. Cheers!"

John took off, leaving Joey and Megan to gaze at each other aghast. Aghast and guilty.

chapter twenty

I t was all our fault!" Megan wailed.

"Hey," said Joey. "Blaming ourselves won't help."

Trey had worked his way out of Megan's pocket and up to her shoulder.

"Stop," he said. "Think. And get some help with thinking. Remember your secret weapon. There are more than two thousand eyes in this place, two thousand ears. Someone will know where Chaz has gone."

Of course. Mice.

"I'll go down to Mouse Hall," Megan told Joey. "You tell his dad."

For a moment Joey hesitated. He so much didn't like that division of responsibility. As he told Megan later, of all the things he'd done in his life, this could be the worst—telling a father that his son was missing and in the hands of the opposition. Whereas dropping down to Mouse Hall, handing over your problem to the mouse machine—that was so much easier.

But Joey knew deep down that Megan would be a better ambassador to the mouse world. Mice on all continents adored her and would pull out the extra ounce of effort that could make all the difference.

Joey was right to think that his job would be bad. Of course it was bad. How could it not be?

He sprinted up the spiral stairs to his parents' sitting room and there they all were, the ex-president and the experts. A footman and a maid were removing the tea things, so Joey couldn't say anything yet. Instead, he circled the room, longing to see a flash of that dark red school blazer, or that black hair, longing to find that John the footman had been wrong. But there was no sign.

He grabbed Jake and pulled him into the bedroom. Susie followed, and both she and Jake collapsed on the bed at the news. The last they'd heard was from Ken—that all three kids were safely in the duke's apartment. But now, Chaz was gone? In the hands of Mr. Peabody and Aunt Flo?

"But why!" wailed Susie. "As a *hostage*? To force his dad to give up?"

"Or just to question him about Coconut Man?" asked Jake.

"That's what Megan's finding out," said Joey, "from the guys in Mouse Hall."

"We can't wait for her," said Susie. "We have to tell the president. Right now."

That was Joey's cue to escape upstairs to his room. He really, really didn't want to be around when Susie and Jake led the ex-president gently into their bedroom, and sat him down, and told him.

Ex-President Pindoran wanted to call the police right then, of course. Jake and Susie tried to get him to hold off for a while, but they ran out of reasons for delay because they couldn't mention mice, couldn't ask him to wait until the guys in Mouse Hall told Megan where his son was.

And they couldn't stop the ex-president as he ran downstairs meaning to storm into the servants' hall to demand that someone use the only phone in this palace to call the police.

But the ex-president never made it. A minute after he'd set off down the spiral stairs he came back, his eyes wide.

"It is too late," he said. "We are locked in."

And indeed the ancient oak door was now shut tight, its

lock strong enough to withstand a whole group of rain forest experts, all pushing together.

It's hard to surprise mice, and when Megan lifted the trapdoor and wriggled her way into Mouse Hall, she found they were expecting her. Yes, their scouts had seen everything. Heard everything.

When Aunt Flo left the servants' hall, she'd told her brother that young Chaz appeared to know a great deal about Coconut Man. Which meant that his father was not, after all, Dr. Patel from Fiji but was most likely Loggocorp's worst enemy: the ex-president of Marisco, who still wielded enormous influence on the island.

Mr. Peabody had promptly telephoned a senior executive at Loggocorp, who was now on his way. After the footman—a quilter in disguise—had collected Chaz from the duke's apartment, the Peabodys had driven him away to meet this executive.

"Their plans for young Chaz are unclear," said the director. "The decision rests with the executive whom they will meet. They may simply try to learn from the boy what his father knows about the identity of Coconut Man, and of his descendants. In the worst case, they may hold Chaz as a bargaining chip, keeping him until the ex-president gives up his campaign to save the forest."

"A hostage?" squeaked Megan. "Then we absolutely have to save him! Where do you think they took him?"

"We will soon be in a position to make that determination," said the director, as Trey translated. "There is always a mouse on duty in Mr. Peabody's car with a Thumbtop, to help us keep track of his movements."

Megan couldn't help reaching out to the director in gratitude—but to do what? You don't tickle directors behind the ear. You probably don't even high-five them, with a tap against a paw. So her hand stopped in midair as the director pointed to one of the Thumbtops on the table.

"All we can do now," he said, "is to wait for our operative to report Mr. Peabody's position."

It was only a few minutes but to Megan it felt like hours as she sat in a corner of Mouse Central, her head in her hands, waiting for the report. It didn't help when a messenger mouse ran in with the news that he'd seen a quilter locking the massive oak door to the South Tower and making off with the key. Didn't help at all.

And it helped even less when a group of muscle mice trundled a packet of cookies toward her that they'd borrowed from the storeroom. Chocolate cookies. Chocky bickies. Megan thought she was going to cry.

Then she sat up sharply, hitting her head on the ceiling but not noticing the pain because the mouse on Thumbtop duty was signaling to the Director of Security, his gestures crisp and somehow grim. Trey ran over to peer at the tiny screen, then sprinted back to Megan.

"The good news is that he's fine," he said. "Chaz is fine. He's in a cottage just outside this estate. They're waiting for the big Loggocorp guy, who's due to arrive in about half an hour. Look. These guys have brought up the map."

Megan ooched over to the big table to peer at the Thumbtop's screen through her magnifying glass.

It was the satellite view of Buckford Hall showing its long, long driveway curling far across fields and woodlands until it joined the public road that encircled the grounds. Near where the driveway ended was a little lane with four cottages. And in front of one of them an exclamation point was flashing on and off. The precise location of Mr. Peabody's car.

Megan sat back, her mind racing. Her first thought was to find a phone and call the police. Or not? If only she could ask her mom, or Jake, if that was a good idea—if only they weren't locked away, with no phones, no Internet. True, she could send a mouse up with a message, but that would use up precious time. And besides—

"You can't call the cops," said Trey, reading her mind. "Think of all the lies you'd have to tell, starting with the lie about how you know where they took Chaz."

Yes, this was like the situation last August, when the Humans Who Knew had been more or less kidnapped by climate deniers. No way they could call the cops without committing a felony—lying to protect the secrets of mice.

Now Trey climbed onto Megan's shoulder and stroked her cheek.

"It'll be okay," he said. "We can get him out ourselves. Do you see what those roofs are made of?"

"Thatch?" said Megan, peering down again at the satellite picture.

"And you know what lives in thatched roofs?"

"Mice?"

"You betcha. They're mouse condos. Very desirable property. I wonder how many guys live there."

An IT mouse quickly found the e-mail address of the clan in the cottage and tapped out his question. How many mice?

About a hundred in this roof, came the reply. Same number in the thatch of the other three cottages.

With a mouse army that big, it should be possible to mount an attack so that a human could rush into the cottage and scoop Chaz up while Mr. Peabody and any other humans were squawking and EEEKing and trying to fend off bites. But it had to happen in the next half hour, before the Loggocorp man arrived and began asking Chaz about his dad's hopes and plans for the forest.

And which human could carry out the rescue?

There wasn't much choice, really. Megan noticed that hundreds of mice were looking at her, waiting. Trey ran up her arm to lean against her neck, as if that would lend her some of his mouseness, the part that thinks and acts at lightning speed in emergencies.

"Let me see that map again," she said.

You could reach the cottage by road, of course, but there was a shorter way—a path that led through the woods. Megan recognized it as the trail she and Joey had ridden on yesterday. She could see the split where the right fork took off for the cliff overlooking the lawns and the left fork led to the road that encircled the estate, joining it near the four cottages.

"How far is it through the woods?" she asked.

A mouse did some quick measuring. Nearly three miles.

Megan took a deep breath and reached up to the comforting form of Trey. No way she could run three miles in half an hour through a dark forest—not on her own legs. But she knew where she could borrow some.

"Are you thinking what I'm thinking?" asked Trey.

Megan nodded. "You'll come with me this time?" she asked.

"Of course," said Trey. "And we should probably take along one of these guys. A muscle mouse. Just in case."

At least ten mice volunteered for the job. Trey picked the one who looked strongest. Then the two mice walked ahead of Megan as she wriggled her way to the trapdoor, calling back over her shoulder, "Tell the guys in the cottage to get ready to attack. The signal will be someone whistling 'God Save the Queen.'"

chapter twenty-one

he stable was quiet except for the soft munching of hay in the dusk, and Megan leaned against the wall for a moment to catch her breath.

She looked at the row of horses. Most of them were full size, and there was no way she could put saddles on them, let alone climb up. It would have to be something shorter—one of the three ponies. But which one? She ruled out Petal, the pony Olivia had been riding, because who knew? It might be hard-wired only to obey Olivia. There was Snowball, Joey's circular mount, but Megan remembered that it had been hard for Joey to find the accelerator before Snowball decided to wallow along in Prince's wake.

So there was only one option. Prince himself. He had plenty of acceleration and legs that could cover three miles in a flash. The downside? Well, that Prince was plainly the boss.

He might or might not follow instructions. Might or might not try to kill her.

Megan went up to Prince's stall and gazed into his eyes. "Will you help me?" she asked. "Will you take me to Chaz? Please?"

Of course horses are not mice, and though their brains might evolve at some point in the future it hasn't happened yet, so there was no way Prince could understand. But at least he looked friendly now, his ears slanting forward as if he was eager for what came next, for anything that would break the monotony of the stable.

Megan was glad that the groom had made her and Joey take off the saddles and bridles themselves, so at least she knew where they were stored. But she had no clue how the bridle went back on. In the half dark it looked like a jumble of straps and buckles that made no sense. She flopped down on the straw of Prince's stall, hoping that nobody had pooped there.

"There's no way," she said. Prince actually bent his head down to nuzzle the bridle in her hands as if he recognized that it was his ticket to an exciting night out. But he couldn't exactly put it on himself.

"Hey, you can't give up now!" said Trey, rushing down her arm. "Put the thing down, and we'll help you."

Megan laid the bridle on the straw and the two mice went to work, spreading it out so she could begin to see what went where.

"This metal thing goes into his mouth first, right?" said Trey, patting the bit. "It must do. Then this strap would go behind his ears, so all you have to do is to buckle *this* strap. . . ."

It was worth a try. Prince let Megan open his mouth and slip the bit between his teeth. And he didn't seem to mind when she bent his ears to push one of the straps behind them, before she did up the buckle. And he stood miraculously still while she put on the saddle and tightened the girth. So far, so good.

She led Prince out into the stable yard, hoping his *clop-clop* wouldn't alert anyone. Then she took a deep breath, stuck a foot in a stirrup and hoisted herself on top, which seemed to be Prince's signal to do a pirouette, then another, and then to take off.

Megan clung to the saddle as she had this morning, feeling she had no chance of slowing Prince down and not much chance of steering him in the right direction.

"Trey!" she said. "Do something!"

"It's okay!" said Trey, holding very tight to a braid. "He's heading for the woods!"

And indeed they had soon left the half light of the evening for the deeper dusk of the woods, galloping along the trail while Megan hung on to the saddle and the two mice clung to braids that swung wild and free.

There was just one problem. One little problem. When they got to the fork in the trail, they must absolutely not take the right turn that led back toward the house, as Prince had done yesterday. They must absolutely turn left.

That fork was coming up fast, and Megan sensed that Prince was already thinking of veering to the right. She tugged on the reins to slow him up, with a stronger tug on the left one—and as they reached the fork, Prince came almost to a stop, prancing and pawing the ground.

Was there a problem with the left trail? Something humans didn't know about? Some long-leggity beastie that came out at night to frighten ponies?

There was just enough light for Megan to see movement in Prince's mane. It was Trey, climbing up to the pony's right ear. Whatever he did worked, because Prince immediately took off to the left.

Trey climbed back up to her shoulder and grabbed a braid again.

"What did you do?" she asked. "Can you *talk* to horses?"

"Course I can," he said. "Doesn't mean they understand. I just said 'Boo,' right into his ear. Works every time."

Now Prince was traveling at a steady canter, and Megan began to get the hang of it. You didn't have to hold on for dear life. Instead you could sit calmly on the saddle, move with the pony, feel you were part of the pony. And the pony seemed to approve, because when they came out of the wood his power steering kicked in, as well as the brakes, and he obeyed Megan's commands when it was most important.

There was just enough light for Megan to see the lane that ran in front of the four thatched cottages. She slowed Prince down so she could slide off him, and led him for the last few yards, walking on a grass verge that cut down on the clip-clop factor. Opposite the cottages she tied his reins to a small tree, then ran across the road to crouch down behind Mr. Peabody's car.

"Can you find out what's happening?" she whispered to Trey.

"Easy peasy," said Trey. "Come on, big guy," he called to the muscle mouse, and the two took off while Megan held her breath. Didn't this sort of fairy-tale cottage always have a cat? Probably a black one, and a witch to go with it?

Now she could see the faint outline of two mouse heads peering into the window beside the front door, a window with drawn curtains that left just enough of a crack for mice to see in. After they had peered, they listened. Megan could see that each of the two mouse outlines had an ear pressed to the windowpane.

In a couple of minutes, Trey was back on her shoulder.

"Chaz is in there, and he seems fine," he said. "Mr. Peabody and Aunt Flo are feeding him cake, and Chaz doesn't even look worried."

That was so good to hear. Good that Chaz wasn't nearly as terrified as he ought to be.

Megan realized that one of her shoulders was empty.

"Where's the other guy? The muscle mouse?"

"He went inside, to scout around," said Trey. "That's one brave dude."

The muscle mouse was soon back, and in the last of the evening light he told them in MSL what he'd heard. Mr. Peabody had been talking to the Loggocorp guy on a phone. It sounded as if he'd be here very soon.

That fact gave Megan the dose of bravery she needed for the next steps. Like creeping up to the front door to test the handle and finding it wasn't locked. Looking up toward the thatched roof while she whistled "My Country, 'Tis of Thee." Watching the roof come alive in the dusk as hundreds of mice scrambled down under the eaves and into the house at the sound of their national anthem, the sound of "God Save the Queen."

Now began a full-throated squawking and EEEEKing from inside as mice jumped on both full-size humans. They didn't bite (mice really don't like the taste of human) but they didn't have to as they tweaked ears and noses and pulled hair and ran up pant legs while an occasional claw prickled a scalp or a neck or a knee.

In the chaos Megan rushed into the cottage, grabbed Chaz by the hand and raced him back to Prince. She heaved him up onto the saddle, then climbed up behind him, holding him tight with one arm while she gave the softest touch to the accelerator, the barest pressure of heels to horse, and aimed Prince for the trail back through the woods.

They were just in time, ducking into the trees as a car came roaring along the road, its tires squealing as it turned into the lane.

Normally Prince, with his built-in GPS, would have headed straight back to the stable, but Trey realized that would be a bad idea.

"The car," he said. "It must have seen us vanishing into the woods. And of course those Peabodys saw you. They might drive back to the house and wait for you by the stables, so just in case . . ."

Yes, just in case, it made excellent sense to avoid the stables. This time, when they came to the split in the path, she persuaded Prince to take the fork that led to the steep bluff, and the bridge over the little river, and a more secret way back to Buckford Hall.

Meanwhile Chaz kept up a rain of questions. Where did all those mice come from? Wasn't he going to see a doctor? Where were they going?

You'll get the answers, she told him. We don't know everything. Just that we're going back to your daddy now. Hush.

When they reached the cliff where Prince had finally stopped his runaway gallop yesterday, Megan slid off, leaving Chaz on top.

"We're playing a game," she said. "We're going to surprise your daddy and all the others. But you have to keep very quiet or you'll spoil the surprise."

"Okay," he whispered.

She led the pony down the steep path that led to the bridge over the little river, then across the lawns toward Buckford

Hall, which looked weird for some reason, looming up in the dark. For a moment she couldn't think what was wrong with the house, then realized that there were no lights. No lights at all, except perhaps a faint glow coming from the second floor of the South Tower. Firelight, perhaps? A candle or two?

Now what? Should she stand below that window and shout? Even though it might make every quilter in the house look outside and see them? Or should she throw gravel at the window? Great idea, except that there was no gravel to be found on this smooth expanse of lawn.

Megan felt mouse feet moving from one shoulder to the other, as if two mice were conferring, even though it was much too dark for MSL.

"This dude knows his way around," whispered Trey. "He can take us to a side door."

"Wait a minute! How can you . . . ?" began Megan before she stopped herself, because she was, after all, in the presence of a Snuggle.

"How can I what?" Chaz asked.

"I was just talking to myself," she said, and this time Trey came very close to her ear to whisper.

"How can we speak MSL in the dark?" he whispered. "We can't. We use DSL—Dark Sign Language. Mouse holes aren't exactly well lit so it's something we learn for emergencies. Prods and jabs and taps—stuff like that. Anyway, once we're inside the house, this guy can help us find a flashlight. And he knows where the keys are kept, so we can unlock the South Tower."

As Megan led Prince across the lawns, she could just make out the dim shape of the gazebo, so she tied the pony to one of its columns and helped Chaz slide down to join her. Then Trey translated the jabs and prods and taps of the muscle mouse's DSL, giving Megan directions to a walled garden at the base of the North Tower. It was the duke's private garden, Trey whispered. And leading from it into the house was a small door that was hardly ever locked.

And yes, when Megan navigated to that door, the handle turned and the door opened. But into what? Inside it was pitch dark. She stood still and waited for mouse help. Then as her eyes adjusted she became aware of a glimmer of light, a faint glow that was just enough to reveal that they were in a room where the duke probably took off his muddy boots, when he had the use of his feet.

She was tiptoeing toward the dim light when Chaz crashed into a little cart, knocking over a potted plant. That brought the dim light closer and stronger until it revealed itself to be a flashlight focused full on her.

chapter twenty-two

ell, well, well, fancy meeting you!" came the voice behind the flashlight. "What a lark, the lights going out! I expect you're playing murder, what? Or hide-and-seek in the dark? Oh, but look at that cut!"

The flashlight had come close enough for Megan to see the duke's dim face behind it in the light reflected off her. Now the beam focused on Chaz's knee, which was a bloody mess. The Band-Aid had come off and he'd made the cut a bit worse when he crashed into the cart.

"Plaster fell off, did it? I'll take you to our first-aid room myself. Find another. And you never did get those chocky bickies, did you, old chap? Can't take you upstairs for a chocky bicky now, because my confounded lift isn't working. I was down here looking for a book in the library when the lights went

For a moment, she froze. Should she run back outside to the walled garden? But Chaz was still on the floor, still untangling himself from the fronds of the plant.

Besides, it was too late.

off. But don't worry, I'm sure they will be back soon. Lucky I always have this torch with me, just in case!"

Megan felt feet climbing down her legs and strained to see where the mouse was going, but the duke's flashlight was shining straight into her eyes. More mouse feet, this time climbing up her back, hidden from the light.

"I sent the muscle mouse off to the South Tower," whispered Trey from behind her neck. "Told him he should get Ken to tell your folks what happened. That Chaz is fine."

"Come along," the duke was saying. "The little man can sit on my lap and hold the torch. For you, young lady, there's a place to stand at the back. John the footman likes to ride there when no one's looking. Peabody says it's not dignified!"

In the dim light Megan could just make out a bar at the back of the wheelchair where she could stand, up against the bag where Sir Quentin had been riding when Chaz cut his knee. Sure enough, she felt a slight wriggling in the bag. Sir Quentin, sticking with his duke.

She had to hold on tight while the duke spun the chair around and zoomed out of the little room and into a maze of passages. When he reached the main corridor at the back of the huge house, he felt free to speed up even more.

"Whee!" he said. "Remember Mr. Toad in *The Wind in the*

Willows? When he drove so fast? Used to read that to my children. *Toot toot!*"

That got a gurgling laugh out of Chaz. "But Mr. Toad kept crashing, didn't he!" he said.

"So he did," said the duke. "But he never crashed in a wheelchair, what?"

He turned sharply into the first-aid room and jammed on the brakes so hard that Chaz shot off his lap. Megan jumped off and picked Chaz up, glad to hear him laughing. Then she took the flashlight he'd been holding and parked it so it shone up at the ceiling and lit the whole room while she found a large Band-Aid and stuck it on Chaz's knee.

"Now we'll take you back to your dad," she said. "As soon as we find the key. The door to that tower got locked, Your Grace," she explained, adding, "Maybe by accident," because she didn't want to be the one to tell the duke his palace had filled up with spies.

"What's that?" said the duke. "Door to the South Tower locked? Don't think that's happened since our civil war. Fifth duke kept some prisoners there. Can't lock those old doors by accident, young woman. Someone's idea of a joke, what? Hop on board, Master Chaz, and I'll take you to our key room."

Chaz climbed back on the duke's knee, and Megan stood

behind him again as the chair moved out, its electric motor making no sound as it slid along the corridor—past the dim glow and the chatter of voices that meant the servants were huddled in their hall by candlelight. Past the broom closet that hid Mouse Hall. Finally into a room where rows of massive keys dangled from high hooks.

Megan dragged over a chair to help her reach the keys and aimed the flashlight at the labels above them. And she felt a deep clunk of disappointment in her stomach.

"I can't see it!" she said, turning—and almost collapsed when she saw a shadowy figure behind the duke, a figure that said, "I was lookin' for you, Your Grace, because there's things goin' on that I don't like at all and I don't understand, to be honest. Like them fuses. I went to try and get the lights back on, but them fuses have all been hid."

"That you, John?" asked the duke. "I say, that's a bit rich! Hiding the fuses! Locking the door! If this is all your brother's doing, young lady, I think he's gone a bit far. Let's find that key, then I'll give young Joseph a piece of my mind."

It took less than a minute for John to track down a six-inch key labeled "ST," then he grabbed a handful of candles and ran ahead to unlock the South Tower. Megan and Chaz sprinted up the spiral stairs into the firelit sitting room and a scene of such joyous relief that almost every human cried a bit. After huge hugs from her mom and Jake, Megan even walked into a surprise hug from Joey, and yes, even his face was a bit damp.

A happy reunion goes only so far, of course. When the hugs had died away, and Chaz was clinging safely to his dad, John the footman ran down with Heinrich and Martin and Pierre to bring the wheelchair upstairs, with the duke still in it.

"Bad show, what?" he said when his wheels touched down. "Not what you expect from a stay at Buckford Hall. Not quite up to our usual standards of hospitality. When I see young Joseph . . ."

Then he saw young Joseph, saw that he'd been locked in with the others, which meant that the fusing of the lights and the locking of the door were much more serious than a twelve-year-old's idea of a joke. And someone had to tell him, more or less, what was going on. But how much?

After a whispered consultation with Sir Brian, Susie and Jake gave His Grace an edited version of the facts, explaining that the quilters were not what they seemed but were men from Loggocorp, an organization hostile to the experts' goals.

"Men?" said the duke. "Men, pretending to be quilters?

Never heard of such a thing! How did they manage to fool Peabody?"

"They didn't," said Jake—and told the duke about Peabody's role: that he seemed to be working for Loggocorp and had been sent here as a spy.

"The bounder!" exclaimed the duke, his cheeks darkening to a deeper pink. "The cad! Came to me with excellent references, promising to help with the tourist business. Filling my house with spies, was he? Wanted my trees? Let's send for the police!"

"Yes, let's do that," said the ex-president, clutching Chaz.

Megan looked at Jake, because if anybody could have thought of a way to get the police involved, without giving away the secrets of mice . . .

Jake must have guessed what she was thinking, because he made the slightest shake of the head. No. Not even now. He was right, of course, because there was no way Megan could explain to the police how she had rescued Chaz without lying.

"Let's hold off on the cops," Jake said. "If we call them now, this place will be crawling with reporters, which would make it hard for you guys to finish your job."

Yes, hard for anyone from Coconut Man's family to secretly approach them, and hard for the whole purpose of the mission to be achieved.

There was one voice that mattered: ex-President Pindoran, who was still holding Chaz tight. "A little delay in informing the police is acceptable," he said, "but these people must surely be punished eventually, after what they did to my son."

"They will be punished," said Jake. "I promise."

Of course. Even if the punishment had to be a secret one, mice would make sure that it happened, and that it was brutal.

"But the house is still full of spies," said Sir Brian. "Evidently our talk about sea levels didn't drive them away as we had hoped. It could be impossible for the gentleman we are expecting to meet us here."

Megan felt mouse feet climbing up to the pocket where Trey was hiding. Gentle pressure, as the pocket took in an extra mouse. Then Trey's "Gotta talk" signal, a sharp jab in her side.

She fished him out of the pocket and held him up to an ear.

"There's a plan," he said. "In the bedroom, now!"

Megan went over to Jake and her mom to whisper, "Mouse plan." She picked up a candle, and Jake and Susie followed her into the bedroom, where Joey joined them. A mouse was sitting on the bed, its eyes reflecting the candlelight. Ken.

"A geezer from Mouse Hall just told me something very interesting," he said. "Perfect way to get them quilters out of your hair, yeah? And send the whole lot into the arms of the law, away from this place."

He waited to make sure he had their full attention.

"Here's what you do," he continued. "You get an army of five thousand blokes to surround this place. Cannons going off. Quilters being told they're doomed unless they scarper. Skedaddle. Get out of here. Something like that work for you?"

chapter twenty-three

I t didn't take Ken long to explain how an army of five thousand men, plus cannons, could sweep the quilters out of Buckford Hall.

It would be a virtual army, with virtual cannons.

As Ken had learned in Mouse Hall, thousands of visitors sat on the Buckford lawns four times every summer for a sound-and-light show, in which the house told its own story. A disembodied voice boomed the narration while lights picked out the parts of the house that the voice was talking about.

"The guys downstairs know that show backwards," said Ken. "They say there's bits that will scare the daylights out of them quilters. And there's ways to pick them bits out."

With their shortage of thumbs, it would be a long, slow job for mice to edit that soundtrack and fish out the scary bits. But a human could do it, fast. So if Mr. Jake could come along to the control room, they'd get started.

"Wait!" said Jake. "There's no electricity!"

"Thought of that, didn't I?" said Ken. "I put it to the chief mouse electrician. 'Whatcher going to do about electricity?' I said. 'Not a problem,' he said. 'Different circuit.' He's checked them fuses and no worries."

That left one little problem, of course. How can you explain to a group of rain forest experts that you've suddenly learned some extremely interesting facts about a sound-and-light show from a very mysterious source?

Joey had the answer. You send for John the footman, and ask him questions about sound-and-light shows, and look surprised at the answers, even though you know them already. Then you all go back into the living room and lay out your plan to the others.

John the footman took the duke's flashlight and led Jake and Joey to the sound-and-light control room, with Trey riding in Joey's pocket to translate, and Sir Quentin in Jake's.

Sir Quentin?

"Bet he knows more about English history than anybody," Jake had whispered to Megan and her mom. "He can help us pick out the best bits."

On the way they called in at a storeroom for more candles,

and it was by the flickering light of a candle that John made his way back to the South Tower, ten minutes later.

"They didn't want me to stick around, for some reason," he said. "But he said it's a lovely setup, your Mr. Fisher did. The bees' knees. And he'll have something for them quilters in fifteen minutes. Something they'll never forget."

Then John took off to warn the palace staff clustered by candlelight in the servants' hall: it was about to get noisy, but they mustn't worry. Those Americans had everything under control.

Once John had left the little control room, Joey and Jake could let themselves be blown away by the mouse power waiting for them. Two media mice told them exactly which switches did what. A psychology mouse was on hand to give his opinion on which parts of the script would be most effective at frightening humans, and three history mice (with some suggestions from Sir Quentin) helped them pick those parts out.

Editing was easy. Jake played the recording, and when he came to a useful phrase a director mouse raised a paw. Jake then pressed the copying key until the paw came down again.

There were parts of that script that could have been written for modern times. Could have been written for quilters. Like one part that dealt with the seventeenth century:

Civil war is raging throughout England. The Duke of Wiltshire and his followers remain loyal to King Charles. But the rebel Roundheads are drawing closer, and reach the woods around Buckford Hall. Imagine that [paw up] *tonight, you are surrounded* [paw down].

Then:

In 1723, a terrible fire ravaged Buckford Hall. The family and all the servants had to [paw up] *come outside* [paw down] to watch in horror. Imagine you must run for your life, [paw up] *leaving all your belongings behind* [paw down].

Easy peasy, except that there wasn't as much useable script as Jake would have liked. But as the humans in the tower could tell when the show began, that didn't matter. Didn't matter at all.

While Jake was gone, the experts got back to the task that had been interrupted by the news of Chaz's disappearance:

polishing their presentation for the descendant of Coconut Man, presuming that he (or she) would still appear, once the quilters had been cleaned out.

Megan and Joey had the job of duke-minders, which meant mostly listening to his worries about Mr. Peabody. How could he have let the house fill with impostors? What was the world coming to?

Suddenly he was interrupted by a loud

BOOM!

A ferocious explosion, the sound of an ancient cannon, echoed through the woods. Then a searchlight carved through the night, so bright that the humans in the tower had to shield their eyes.

And that was just the beginning.

Ten more lights came into play, illuminating one part of the house and then another, probing deep into its windows. Did Megan see the flash of a human face at one of them? Someone with an arm up to shield his eyes, trying to peer through the impossible glare to the woods beyond?

Now came the voice. A booming voice with a sort of electronic "wah wah" between some of the phrases, hiding the fact that sentences weren't continuous:

"*Tonight you are surrounded* [wah wah] *come outside* [wah wah] *leaving all your belongings behind. . . .*"

There was a short silence while the lights still darted and probed. Then the voice came again. "*We are waiting* [wah wah] *soon* [wah wah] *we will attack.*"

Megan's eyes were on the front door of the huge house—and yes, there were shapes under the portico, quilters hanging back in there, indecisive, needing one more push.

It came in the form of a different voice, but one with the sort of breathiness you get when someone is speaking softly with his (or her) mouth very close to a microphone. A voice that didn't sound quite human.

"Please be aware," it said, "that canisters of tear gas are ready to be released. Those of you who delay your departure may be driven out in ignominy, driven out like RATS!"

Megan glanced at her mom and could see her hand was to her mouth in amazement. Sir Quentin?

"As you progress down the driveway no harm will befall you," said the voice. "But if you delay, then we cannot vouch for the consequences. Go now, I tell you, NOW!"

There was another loud boom, this one seeming to come from deep inside Buckford Hall.

First a quilter emerged from the front door and started running down the hill, holding up his skirt with one hand and using the other to shield his eyes from the continuing glare of the lights. Then another man, this one in a frilly pink shirt. And another wearing a tight leopard-skin dress.

Then came the next batch, and . . .

"Mom, look!" said Megan.

In this group was one figure who looked like a genuine middle-aged woman, holding by the hand a slightly overweight girl of about nine, running as fast as her stubby legs could carry her.

"It's that girl!" said Chaz. "That girl who wanted to play."

Olivia, with her Aunt Flo.

The duke's wheelchair was parked at a window, and Megan glanced at him from time to time, glad to see he was smiling more and more broadly beneath his bristly white mustache.

"Jolly good show," he said. "Don't know how Fisher did it, a Yank like him, putting in that extra part. Managed to sound quite English, what?"

"It must be the microphone," said Megan's mom. "Special effects."

"Newfangled gadgets!" said the duke. "What will they think of next? Mrs. Fisher, Susie, do you think your husband would record the whole script for me? With those special effects?"

At this point, after a day of such peaks and valleys, it

didn't take much to finish Susie off, and to the duke's surprise, to everyone's surprise, she could hardly talk through her laughter—imagining Jake at the microphone, as she told Megan later, with big ears and whiskers. Jake as Sir Quentin.

"I know he'd love to," she finally managed to say. "It would be the high point of his life."

The first job after the quilters had left was to restore electricity to the house, which wasn't easy until the fuses were found.

"Why would the quilters hide them?" asked Joey.

His dad shrugged. "To make sure no one put them back, I guess," he said. "Maybe they were planning to sneak into our tower to listen in the dark."

With all the quilters far away by now, there was no one to lead them to the fuses. No one, that is, until a mouse ran up to Trey with a message for Megan, who crossed her fingers and wrapped the message in a nice little lie.

"When we came in at the side door," she said, "I saw something gleaming in one of the boots in that room. Big rubber boots."

She led a couple of rain forest experts and John the footman to the little room full of boots, quite anxious about whether the things they were looking for actually "gleamed," because who knew about British fuses?

They were just where the messenger had said they would be—not gleaming but white, which was close enough. It didn't take long for John and the experts to carry the boots to the big fuse box near the butler's pantry, and push them back into place to bring the lights of the massive house on again, section by section.

As the group headed back to the South Tower, a mouse darted out from behind a pink satin couch and scrambled up to Megan's shoulder. Trey.

"Guy from Mouse Hall has something to tell you," he said. "He's in Mr. Peabody's office. Bring Jake."

Megan tugged on Jake's sleeve to hold him back, then she led him to the office, where a messenger from Mouse Hall gave instructions. Jake should use the one phone in the palace—Mr. Peabody's phone—to send an anonymous tip to the police telling them to watch out for certain license numbers. They'd be particularly interested in Mr. Peabody's car because—surprise, surprise—he'd made a habit of robbing English aristocrats and was wanted under a number of different names.

Oh, and the police should definitely stop the bus full of men dressed as women, among whom were certain criminals known to the police for their skill in planting listening devices.

After he'd made his report to the police, Jake called a couple of tabloid newspapers (on Mouse Hall's advice), telling them of the expected arrests. And why would the papers be interested in what sounded like normal police routine? How about the arrest of a man who had robbed some of the loftiest in the land, fiddling the accounts at the stateliest of homes? How about a busload of young executives from a mighty international corporation who'd have a hard time explaining why they'd been caught in very bad company, all dressed as women?

It was while Jake was on the last of these calls that a second messenger mouse appeared and said something to Trey that looked urgent. And to judge by Trey's reaction, astonishing.

"Wait, wait, wait," he said. "Are you sure? Really? Up there?"

More signs, until Trey seemed satisfied enough to relay the message to Megan.

"Ready for goose bumps?" he whispered. "Seems the great-great-grandson of Coconut Man is in your parents' room. Now. Sort of hidden. And you shouldn't tell anyone else. Not yet."

Yes, of course that brought goose bumps. Gigantic goose bumps. How could it not? There was no way a real human could have made it into the house through all that noise and light. Surely in the chaos of the evening only a supernatural presence could have drifted out of myth and legend and into the South Tower?

chapter twenty-four

Megan raced up the spiral stairs and quickly scanned the room. The scene was just as she'd left it, except that now the lights were on, revealing the duke in deep conversation with Laura on the problems faced by lemurs. No sign of a visitor, not even a ghostly hint of one.

Megan made herself go look in the bedroom, but no one was there but Ken.

"Looking for a certain great-great-grandson, are you?" he asked with a huge grin. "Here's what you want." He waved toward a messenger mouse who was sitting on the bed.

Megan glared at Trey. Had he lied when he promised her a living, breathing heir to Coconut Man? She unstrapped the Thumbtop from the messenger's back, pulled out her magnifying glass and looked at the screen. Nothing there but a story, starting with "Once upon a time."

"You're meant to read it aloud," said Trey.

"I'm meant to *what*?" she asked.

"Trust me," he said. "Do it."

Megan went into the next room, where everyone looked busy, as if they had much more important things to do than to listen to some kid reading them a fairy tale.

She took a deep breath.

"Hey," she said, and felt herself starting to get a bit pink when everyone stopped talking and gazed up at her. "I'm going to read you a story."

The adults looked at each other with expressions ranging from annoyed to indulgent. Only Chaz showed any enthusiasm.

"Oh goody!" he said, sitting on the floor in front of her. "Story time."

Megan peered at the Thumbtop's screen through her magnifying glass.

"Once upon a time," she began, "an Englishman came to the island of Marisco. He was the captain of a British naval ship."

Now she had everyone's attention. Big time. Susie and Jake both hurried over to Megan's side, their eyes wide. Megan handed the Thumbtop to her mom, who peered through her own magnifying glass as she took over the story.

"The Englishman drove off a band of pirates from the coast of Marisco," she read. "In gratitude, the ruler gave this captain the deed to much of the forest that covered the western part of the island. The captain and his crew stayed for a few weeks, enjoying the Mariscans' hospitality and the beauty of the island. Unfortunately, one afternoon when the captain was sitting in the shade of a palm tree, a coconut fell on his head. He lost his memory and wandered off into his forest. His crew searched for him diligently, but after a week they gave up and sailed away."

"Coconut Man!" breathed Chaz.

"Yes, Coconut Man," said Susie, and carried on with the story—how Coconut Man stayed on the island for many years while legends grew around him. Tales of good deeds, like saving a boy from drowning and pulling an old man from a burning hut.

Chaz leapt to his feet to say, "He still does good deeds!"

"Yes," said the ex-president. "Hush."

Susie had skimmed ahead to see where the story was going, and she grinned at Chaz. "His spirit lives on in Marisco, but Coconut Man himself went away. Listen to this."

She told how one day another British ship arrived, and its crew hunted everywhere for Coconut Man. He hid from them for days, but finally the sailors spotted him high up in a tree and dragged him to their ship. Why?

At this point in the story Susie went to stand behind the duke and put a hand on his shoulder.

"Coconut Man's older brother had died in a hunting accident, falling from his horse," she read. "And Coconut Man had inherited his title. He was now the twelfth Duke of Wiltshire."

It was lucky that the sixteenth Duke of Wiltshire was safely in his wheelchair, because there was enough shock on his face to fell any vertical nobleman. His color went from pink to a full red, and for a moment he looked as if it was hard to catch his breath.

"Frederick!" he said finally. "You've solved the mystery of Frederick! My great-great-grandfather. We always heard he was a bit addled, don't you know. Wrong in the head. Hit by a coconut, was he? That's rich. I say old chap, are you all right?"

Ex-President Pindoran had leapt to his feet and bounded over to grab the duke's hand.

"You!" was all the ex-president could say. "You are the heir to Coconut Man. Our real mission here is to save the rain forest. And the forest is yours."

There was one thing the rain forest group still needed, of course. Proof. Something that would stand up in court against the expensive lawyers of Loggocorp.

"Do you think your great-great-grandfather left any evidence?" asked Sir Brian. "Some proof that he owned the forest?"

"Like something in your family papers?" prompted Susie. "Memoirs? Diaries? Letters?"

It was John the footman who spoke.

"Maybe there's something in that there cupboard in the library, Your Grace," he said. "Full of old papers, it is."

"Well, at least we can have a look-see," said the duke. "Take me downstairs, John, there's a good chap."

Heinrich, Jake, and Pierre helped John carry the wheelchair down the stairs, then everyone ran to keep up as the duke motored quickly to the library and parked in front of a tall closet. Then Megan saw the eagerness in the experts' faces evaporate. The door to the closet was open, and the papers in it were in total disarray, as if they'd been taken out and shoved back in no particular order.

"Peabody," said Jake sadly. "Looks as if he got here first."

It was then that a mouse ran up Megan's arm. Sir Quentin.

"Observe those canines," he whispered.

Megan noticed that one section of the wall was free of books, giving space to portraits of six dogs.

"Does not the animal on the left bear a strong resemblance to the pet in the portrait of the twelfth duke?" asked Sir Quentin. "And is there not something strange about its gaze?"

Yes, that spaniel—the one with three colors in its coat. Megan remembered it now from two nights ago, when the duke had pointed to the ancestor with a naval uniform and a faraway look—clutching that dog. In this portrait, one of the dog's eyes was a bit shinier than you'd normally expect.

Megan moved closer to the wall, then did something she had been taught you must never, ever do: she reached out and poked the painting squarely in the eye.

The spaniel swung outward, revealing a small safe.

"Well, knock me over with a feather," said the duke. "Always did think there was something odd about that painting. Now we know, what? Must have been one of Frederick's little jokes."

He wheeled over to the safe, where they could now see a rusty box with "12" painted on the lid. John fetched some tools to force the lid, and there it was. A document, yellow with age, chewed at the corners as if by termites, smeared in places as if by seawater.

"May I?" asked ex-President Pindoran.

As delicately as he could, he lifted the document out of the box, and smiled broadly.

"It is written in the classic Mariscan language of years past," he said. "And it reads, 'I, Gavilan, Ruler of Marisco, give to Lord Frederick and his descendants the rights to our Western Forest until the end of time.'"

. . . .

Now was the time for the presentation that the experts had been polishing, off and on, all day—the presentation that would persuade the heir to Coconut Man to preserve his forest.

They sat around the table in the middle of the library and took turns. Megan was glad to see that the duke kept smiling and nodding in agreement as first Laura made her case for a wild forest where lemurs could continue to live in peace. Then Pierre pointed out that if the woods were left intact, botanists would surely discover new species of plants—plants that might provide miracle cures for many diseases. Heinrich described the amazing diversity of animal life in forests such as the one in Marisco, which probably hid species that had never before been seen. Martin spoke most eloquently of the need for forests to soak up the carbon in the atmosphere and help put the brakes on climate change.

Then came Sir Brian, who told the duke that by saving this forest in its natural state, His Grace would set an example to the world and encourage activists in many countries to stand up to those who wanted to profit by cutting their trees.

Finally, ex-President Pindoran made an eloquent speech about the benefits to Marisco of leaving the rain forest intact, under the care of a foundation run by the Mariscan people—a foundation that would hire wardens to protect the forest, and build an education center, and attract a carefully controlled number of tourists.

"And there is something else," the ex-president added. "Many people in my country feel that the spirit of Coconut Man still lives in the woods and must not be disturbed. You, as his heir, can make sure that his spirit lives on."

All eyes were on the duke, who was gazing at the tabletop with a slight smile.

"Well, well, well," he said finally. "Imagine that. Could be a godsend, what? A forest that I could sell for millions of pounds. I could pay all my bills in one go. Wouldn't have to bother with all those tourists and conferences."

Megan held her breath, and noticed that her mother was clutching Jake's hand.

"But it wouldn't do to get rich that way," the duke went on. "We can't give in to bounders like Loggocorp or Corpolog or whatever they call themselves, can we? Filling my house with spies. Pretending to be quilters. Ridiculous. Besides," he added, reaching out to pat Chaz, who was sitting on his father's knee. "Your Coconut Man would come back to haunt me if I sold his beloved forest."

"So . . ." began Sir Brian.

"So just tell me what you want me to do," said the duke.

"Your foundation—sounds like a good idea to me. As long as you don't expect me to pay for it, what?"

Megan could feel her pocket rotating as a mouse did a pirouette. Both Jake and Susie stood up for pirouettes of their own, while those who hadn't learned to rejoice in the style of mice clapped or stood or raised their fists in the air or yipped or shouted "Ja wohl" or "Très bien" or "Good on you" or "Jolly good show."

chapter twenty-five

There were loose ends, of course, though the question of what happened to Mr. Peabody and the quilters wasn't loose for very long. News about them came from the Director of Security for the Buckford clan, who appeared in the South Tower just before the humans went down to dinner.

"We have heard from clans in two police stations," he said.

Mice at a police station in Basingstoke, halfway to London, reported that the cops had stopped Mr. Peabody's car and arrested him as a fugitive who was wanted for crimes under many different names. He had been Mr. Prendergarst when he worked for the Earl of Uckfield, robbing him blind, and Mr. Clotworthy when he cooked the books of Lord Barton of Ludlow.

And the quilters? News of their fate had arrived from mice in Bagshot, a bit closer to London. Acting on an anonymous tip, police had stopped the bus full of men in women's clothes and removed the five who were wanted by the police for hacking, or bugging, or just plain burglary.

"The rest, the 'Loggocorp Ladies,' underwent the ordeal of facing a battery of reporters and cameramen," said the director. "We have heard from our contacts in certain newspaper offices that they are to be mocked mercilessly in the press, to an extent that they may never live down."

He turned to go, but Megan's mom had one more question.

"Now that you are here," she said, "perhaps you can tell us. How did you mice mess things up so badly? You let us walk straight into a trap!"

The director made the sign for "Slight smile."

"Such an explanation is above my pay grade," he said. "I suggest that you reserve your questions until your return to Cleveland, where our leader will, I am sure, explain the sequence of events. Meanwhile there is a Shakespeare play with a title that sums up the situation."

"*The Comedy of Errors*?" suggested Susie.

"*Much Ado About Nothing*?" guessed Jake.

"Hardly," said the director. "It was *All's Well That Ends Well* that I had in mind."

. . . .

The duke had invited everyone to dine with him, though dinner was nothing like the first occasion—was it only two nights ago?

Someone had laid out food on the sideboard so people could help themselves to cold roast beef and mashed potatoes, and cold Brussels sprouts, but it would take more than a cold Brussels sprout to dampen the experts' mood.

Jake told the group what he had learned from a "friend" who had good contacts in the police force. How the quilters—and Loggocorp—were about to be thoroughly embarrassed by the British press. How Mr. Peabody had been arrested for the repeat offenses of stealing from the aristocracy.

"The bounder," said the duke. "Forged his references, did he? At least he didn't steal from me, as far as I can tell! Didn't need to, what? Expected a big payoff from Loggocorp."

It was Laura who came out with the obvious question.

"How come Loggocorp planted him here in the first place?" she asked.

"They must have known all along that the duke was the heir to Coconut Man," said Jake. "Then they put him here to report if anyone else found out the truth. Like us."

"But how did Loggocorp know it?" asked Martin. "That Coconut Man became the Duke of Wiltshire?"

"I think I can guess," said ex-President Pindoran. "Shortly after the generals took power, and began negotiating with Loggocorp, they set up a national archive of all documents relating to my country, and now I know why. They found what they wanted: evidence of the true identity of Coconut Man."

"Good old Frederick," said the duke. "We should drink a toast to him, don't you think?"

A footman brought champagne for the adults, and everyone stood except the duke, in his wheelchair, and ex-President Pindoran, who had Chaz asleep on his knee.

"To my great-great-grandfather," said the duke, raising his glass toward the portrait of the twelfth duke, the naval officer who had a faraway look in his eyes, as if he saw something that was hidden from most humans.

"To Coconut Man," said Sir Brian.

There were two pieces of unfinished business. The first came with the cold sponge pudding, when the duke lamented the fact that on top of everything else, Mr. Peabody had failed miserably in the job for which he was hired.

"Chap said he'd double my tourist business," said the duke. "It's worse than before he came!"

"We can help with that," said Susie. "We have good contacts, so we can send thousands of Americans your way."

"Excellent!" said the duke. "You Yanks are good at that sort of thing, aren't you."

Well, maybe not all Yanks. But Yanks with the power of a billion mice behind them? You bet.

The second piece of unfinished business was the new audio track for the duke's sound-and-light show. With Sir Quentin in his pocket, Jake made his way back to the control room. John the footman offered to help, but Jake said he got nervous with people around. He'd rather be alone.

And once they were on their own, as he told the rest of his family later, Sir Quentin was awesome, his voice dipping and soaring, soft then loud, far better than the original human voice had been.

The four Humans Who Knew took a different apartment in London for the three days that remained before their flight back to Cleveland. Now at last they and their mice could be tourists, with Ken as their guide.

True, you don't exactly need a guide to find Buckingham Palace or the Tower of London, but Ken knew things from the London Mouse News Network that no previous humans had heard. Like what the Queen *really* thought about the prime minister, and if she'd *really* enjoyed the singing and dancing at the latest royal performance.

On their last night, the four humans went to Sir Brian's apartment to discuss their next move. Ex-President Pindoran was there with Chaz, who was no longer wearing his school uniform.

"My son is coming back with me to Marisco," said the president. "After that scare, I have no wish to be separated from him."

With the help of Trey and Julia, Chaz and Megan played one last game of "God Save the/'Tis of Thee" while the adults discussed the next steps, which would mostly involve money. Money to win the lawsuit that would happen if the generals fought the duke's claim. Money for the lemur sanctuary, and the research labs, and the educational center, and the wardens.

And where would this money come from? Once again, eyes swiveled toward Susie and Jake, because Americans were good at fund-raising, right?

Jake and Susie promised that they would give it their best shot. They looked surprisingly confident, actually.

. . . .

The humans were tired that night when they got back to their apartment, but no one could go to bed yet because of the date that had sneaked up on them. October twenty-sixth. Megan Day. The day mice would celebrate at precisely two o'clock California time, because that was when Megan had signed the Treaty Between the Species and the members of the Mouse Council had all attached their pawprints.

Which meant ten o'clock at night in London.

Jake had set up a corner of the rented apartment for a videoconference so Megan could make her speech, live, to one or two billion mice. And even though she'd learned her speech backward and forward, just looking at that corner, all lit up and ready, gave her that ominous beginning of warmth in her cheeks.

She'd expected it would be a strain, sitting through the whole show, waiting for her turn. But to her surprise—to everyone's surprise—the show was awesome, much better than they'd expected.

The Youth Chorus was word perfect. The Mousettes had learned some amazing moves, including the tallest mouse pyramid ever. Mice from the Theater Club at the factory reenacted great moments in mouse history, like Trey's first contact with Megan, and the mouse raid that he led on Joey's house. Sir Quentin's ode was fine. He'd been a little miffed, as he put it, to learn that the Big Cheese had shortened it. But he'd cheered up again when he was asked to record four new lines in a private videoconference:

Fierce rode she, our Miss Megan, through the night
And rescued Master Chaz from his dire plight.
The claims of coconuts, that's at the core
To keep the forest whole for ever more.

When it was time for Larry's sports report, Megan noticed that Joey had shrunk down into the cushions of the couch and half covered his eyes, afraid that Larry would embarrass himself and bore the fur off the billions of watching mice, as only he could do. But Joey sat forward again as the new comedy routine unfurled, with Savannah pretending to be dumb while Larry played straight mouse:

Savannah: Tell me how Cleveland beat the red underwear team in baseball?

Larry: It's Red Sox, not underwear!

Savannah: But Cleveland won by two points?

Larry: Not points! Runs!

Savannah: Who are Cleveland's best running fronts?

Larry [paws outstretched in frustration]: That's in *football* and it's running *backs*, not fronts.

And so on until (Megan could imagine) mice in the farthest corners of the world were rolling in fits of mouse giggles.

When her own turn came? The moment she'd been dreading for weeks? Maybe it was because the show was so good. Maybe it was because so much had happened in the past week that was even more frightening than public speaking. For whatever reason, Megan found that she could smile into the webcam without that dreaded glow in her cheeks. She could say with conviction (because she meant it) how glad she was to have been the right human in the right place at the right time, and to have written the treaty that brought the two species together permanently.

chapter twenty-six

A t the airport, the humans ran their arrival ritual in reverse. They dropped off the mice at the loading bay behind the terminal, with fond farewells to Ken. And in the long, long passage that led to the plane, Megan again put down her backpack near the poster proclaiming that London was the capital of the world as she pretended to tie her shoe. Then she carried her slightly heavier backpack onto the plane.

There were huge comfort huddles waiting at the Cleveland airport, of course.

Uncle Fred's comfort huddles for humans were bone crushing, and when they were safely inside his car, Julia vanished into a huddle with Curly and Larry that was so intense that it looked, as always, like one mouse with three tails and six ears.

Savannah leapt straight for Susie, making her giggle as her pink straw hat tickled Susie's neck.

"These guys were worried about you," said Uncle Fred. "We all were. The Big Cheese gave me a briefing every day. Blow by blow, disaster by disaster. Like when you did that horse stunt, Megan. Didn't your mother ever tell you not to ride a strange horse through a forest at night?"

Yes, from the safety of Cleveland, it did sound crazy. Through the haze of jet lag, almost everything about their trip sounded crazy.

A messenger mouse was waiting at The Fishery. There was to be a formal meeting between the Big Cheese and his humans in ten minutes' time precisely.

Ten minutes! Yes, that *was* kind of soon for humans with jet lag. In fact the Director of Human Psychology had tried to persuade his boss to postpone the meeting, at least for a couple of hours.

"But I want to see them," said the Big Cheese. "I've missed them."

"Ah," said the director, because he was too surprised to say more. He'd read plenty about patterns of attachment among humans, of course, but for his own leader to make such a confession?

The Big Cheese didn't make that confession to his actual

humans, when they flopped, tired and wrinkled, on the office couch. That wouldn't do at all.

"I am relieved that you have survived your various ordeals," he began. "The trip was indeed rather more exciting for you than I expected."

"Exciting!" said Susie, who was the human most likely to talk back to the Big Cheese. "It was close to being a total disaster, and you let us walk right into it. You must have known that Peabody was in league with Loggocorp. You must have guessed we'd be surrounded by spies."

There was total silence. Megan wished she could read the Big Cheese's expressions, but except on Talking Mice, who can learn facial expressions like "joy," "regret," and "embarrassment" for extra credit, most mouse faces don't reflect what is going on inside.

Then to her relief, the Big Cheese made the sign for "Slight smile."

"We knew about Peabody," he said, "but I let the situation run its course for two reasons. First, it was important for you to act naturally."

Megan glanced at her mom because, yes, Susie Fisher might have had a hard time behaving naturally around Peabody if she'd known he was a bad guy. She'd never been good at faking the way she felt.

"And second?" prompted Jake.

"Acting on the advice of my Director of Human Psychology, I wanted Peabody to reveal his own villainy," he said. "Was it not the evidence of his betrayal that convinced the duke to support your proposal? Rather than enrich himself through a deal with Loggocorp?"

"You're right," said Jake admiringly. "That certainly helped persuade the duke. Knowing Peabody was a cad. A bounder."

"Yes, but—" began Susie.

"But did things spin a little bit out of mouse control?" said the Big Cheese. "I must admit that to some extent they did. However, thanks to the heroic actions of Miss Megan, the situation was saved, and I think we can all agree, in Shakespeare's words—"

To his surprise, Jake and Joey groaned, while Megan and her mom finished his sentence:

"All's well that ends well."

Except that it wasn't yet ended.

"There are still two tasks ahead of us, as I see it," said the Big Cheese. "We need to raise money for the support of Mr. Pindoran's Foundation. We should also get millions upon millions of humans from all over the world to *demand* that the rain forest be preserved. To put so much pressure on the generals—and on Loggocorp—that they give up any thought of a lawsuit and acknowledge the duke's ownership of the forest. We propose to kill both cats with one stone, by going viral."

He paused to let those words sink in and then waved to a media-mouse, who brought up a list on the big monitor in the corner.

What You Need to Go Viral on YouTube
1. Immature humans
2. A catchy tune
3. A celebrity
4. Cute young animals, such as lemurs
5. An "OOPS" moment

Preparations for Operation Viral didn't take long. First, Sir Quentin wrote a song that turned out to be quite sprightly, as if his English experience had knocked all the iambic pentameters out of him. President Pindoran arranged for the most popular composer in Marisco to write the music, while the rain forest experts lined up children's choirs in each of their countries. Joey did the same thing in Cleveland, where he'd sung in the Lakeview Middle School Chorus until his voice started going weird.

That took care of Items 1 and 2—the immature humans and the sprightly tune. And the celebrity for Item 3? It was Daisy Dakota, of course, whose work on Creaturebook made her the most important Snuggle for the Mouse Nation. Daisy was delighted to fly with Susie to Marisco, where they were whisked off to find a lemur group in the rain forest.

Soon the mouse editing team in the Media Department was busy turning pieces of video from all corners of the world into one polished segment. Two weeks after his humans had returned from England, the Big Cheese proclaimed that his nation was ready for Operation Viral. Ready for V-day. And Jake posted the video on YouTube.

First, Daisy Dakota appeared, walking through the rain forest. Brilliantly colored butterflies floated by. Flashes of red and turquoise and yellow sparked above her head as birds flitted through the treetops. Daisy pushed her way carefully past rich thickets of plants, with leaves of all imaginable shades of green, flowers of astonishing shapes and colors.

"Can you imagine," asked Daisy, "cutting all this down?"

At that moment she tripped on a hidden log (as had been planned) and landed, *splat*, in a patch of mud. Oops.

Daisy sat up laughing, as (with some clever editing) three young lemurs came down from the trees to inspect her. So cute.

And while Daisy told the audience about the campaign to

save this beautiful rain forest, there came the first soft humming of a very catchy tune, followed by a burst of sound as the video cut to a choir of children from Marisco (with Chaz in the front row) singing:

> *Hey you, world, now listen to us please.*
> *We're asking you, we're begging you:*
> *Save our trees!*

The next three lines had a different rhythm, and children's choirs from Germany, France, Ghana, England, and Australia took turns singing them:

> *We need the trees as habitat*
> *For bees and bugs and birds.*
> *We need them so lemurs and such*
> *Can frolic there in herds.*
> *We need the woods for beauty*
> *With their plants of every hue.*
> *We need them for the planet*
> *As they suck up CO_2.*
> *We're heading for disaster*
> *If you take away the trees.*

The next lines came from the Lakeview Middle School Chorus in Cleveland, where a sixth grader with red braids stood next to a pale girl with glasses, while in the back row a tall seventh grader opened and shut his mouth but didn't dare make sounds because he had no clue whether they would come out high or low. This chorus sang:

> *So help us save the forest—*
> *Help us, please!*

The video ended with a close-up of a grinning Chaz, impossibly cute because he'd just lost a front tooth.

Oh, and there was the address of the Foundation that would fight to keep the forest intact and maintain it as a resource for research and education, a resource for the world.

On the morning of V-day, when the video was scheduled to go viral, Daisy Dakota had posted news about it on her Creaturebook page, and a few million of her fans followed the link. Next, she put it on her Facebook page. Millions more clicks. More kids learned about the video from her Twitter feed, retweeted a gazillion times. By the end of the day, millions upon millions of Daisy's fans had found the link online, or just spread the word the old-fashioned way, by telling at least six of their friends. From two million to five million. Eight million. Fifty million. A hundred million. . . .

Many of those who saw the video sent money, which went straight to the Foundation, because as it turned out, there was no expensive lawsuit to pay for. In the country of Luxembourg, where Loggocorp had its headquarters, the chief executive officer made a speech to explain why he'd decided not to sue.

From now on (he told his shareholders) the company would stay away from wild forests, and all future harvesting of timber would be sustainable. They would forget Marisco. With the attention of the whole world now squarely on that island's forests, any timber company that dared touch a single tree there would plainly be reviled, with a resultant drop in its share price.

Some people noticed that the CEO looked a little, well, haunted as he made this speech, and for some reason had a tinge of green in his hair, of the sort you might get if some spooky presence puts dye on your hairbrush.

In Marisco, it was rumo   that the generals were also haunted by some magical   aybe the ghost of Coconut Man. A month afte   l they resigned, and amid much rejo   va restored to power.

At Buckfor   d in, after some

amazing publicity in American newspapers. That sound-and-light show? Top of the "must see" list.

Back in Cleveland, Megan and Emily decided to keep singing with the Lakeview Middle School Chorus, and sometimes hung out together after school. Emily was much more fun to be with now, because guess what? Someone had mysteriously found the perfect job for her dad, who was now working at City Hall to keep hackers at bay. As Emily told Megan, he didn't even remember applying for the job. He just got a call one day to tell him that he'd been hired.

And Emily's brother? Another mystery! Somehow he got a scholarship to a military school. He hated it at first, but he adjusted, and was soon doing well without cheating.

"Thank you, sir," Megan said to the Big Cheese at one of the first Tuesday meetings after V-day.

"For what?" he asked, but she noticed his paws going up to the corners of his mouth as if he couldn't help grinning, because there's nothing that mice can't do, right? All's well that ends well.

Mission accomplished.